"Make It Quick."

"Fiesty all of a sudden, aren't you?" Jake taunted, strolling to within inches of her. "Or is your show of temper an act?" he wondered aloud. "Why are you afraid of me, Gayle?"

"I'm not!" Gayle denied hotly—much too hotly. Forcing herself to meet his eyes, she was lured, then caught by the sea-green snare. Beginning to shiver, needing to put distance between them, she backed away from him.

Jake slowly stalked her retreating form. When her spine made contact with the mantlepiece, Gayle cried in desperation, "What do you want of me, Jake?"

Dear Reader,

Although our culture is always changing, the desire to love and be loved is a constant in every woman's heart. Silhouette Romances reflect that desire, sweeping you away with books that will make you laugh and cry, poignant stories that will move you time and time again.

This summer we're featuring Romances with a playful twist. Remember those fun-loving heroines who always manage to get themselves into tricky predicaments? You'll enjoy reading about their escapades in Silhouette Romances by Brittany Young, Debbie Macomber, Annette Broadrick and Rita Rainville.

We're also publishing Romances by many of your all-time favorites such as Ginna Gray, Dixie Browning, Laurie Paige and Joan Hohl. Your overwhelming reaction to these authors has served as a touchstone for us, and we're pleased to bring you more books with Silhouette's distinctive medley of charm, wit and—above all—*romance*. I hope you enjoy this book, and the many stories to come.

Sincerely,

Rosalind Noonan
Editor
SILHOUETTE BOOKS

SRRL-7/85

JOAN HOHL
The Scent of Lilacs

Silhouette Romance

Published by Silhouette Books New York

America's Publisher of Contemporary Romance

For
Pat Smith, for getting me
into this in the first place,
and
Alicia Condon, for keeping me on
track while I polished the work.
Thanks, ladies!

SILHOUETTE BOOKS
300 E. 42nd St., New York, N.Y. 10017

Copyright © 1985 by Joan Hohl

Distributed by Pocket Books

ISBN: 0-373-08376-9

First Silhouette Books printing August, 1985

10 9 8 7 6 5 4 3 2 1

America's Publisher of Contemporary Romance

Printed in the U.S.A.

Books by Joan Hohl

Silhouette Special Edition
Thorne's Way #54

Silhouette Intimate Moments
Moments Harsh, Moments Gentle #35

Silhouette Romance
A Taste for Rich Things #334
Someone Waiting #358
The Scent of Lilacs #376

JOAN HOHL

a Gemini and an inveterate daydreamer, says she always had her head in the clouds. Though she reads eight or nine books a week, she only discovered romances ten years ago. "But as soon as I read the first one," she confesses, "I was hooked." Now an extremely popular author, she is thrilled to be getting paid for exactly what she loves doing best. Joan Hohl also writes under the pseudonym Amii Lorin.

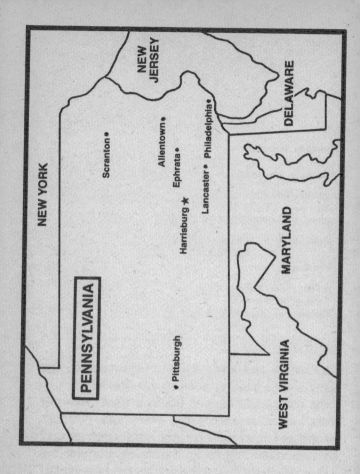

Chapter One

It was raining . . . again. Huddled beneath her umbrella, hunched inside her raincoat, Gayle d'Acier hurried to the parking lot where, for a sizable monthly fee, she parked her compact car while at work.

Gayle d'Acier did not need to work. And for nearly three years she had not. Gayle was a widow—a rather wealthy one. She would have preferred abject poverty and a living husband. In the short amount of time they had been married, Louis d'Acier had become the embodiment of everything good in the world for Gayle. Now Louis was gone. Gayle shivered in the rain.

After the usual frustration of fighting the late-afternoon traffic crawling out of Philadelphia, Gayle sighed in tired relief as she steered the car onto the driveway of her property. Reducing speed, she ran a sweeping glance over the clean lines of the wood-and-glass structure Louis had designed. The house was beautiful, and Gayle loved it.

Another soft sigh whispered through her lips as her gaze skimmed over the large blue and white "For Sale" sign posted on the wide expanse of front lawn.

Gayle's decision to sell the house had not been an easy one. Some of the happiest moments of Gayle's life had occurred within those walls of wood and glass. There were times, late at night, when she fancied she could hear Louis laughing. At those times the pain of loss grew most intense, threatening her very sanity. Gayle knew she had no choice but to sell the house.

To date there had been several prospective buyers interested in the property, but no one had made a firm offer. The selling price was enormous, but in Gayle's opinion, the house was worth every cent. Louis had not only designed the house, using all his considerable talent, he had also lovingly monitored every inch of its construction. Gayle would not lower her asking price by as much as one dollar.

As she maneuvered the car carefully around the curving driveway, Gayle touched the button on the remote control to activate the automatic garage door. The wide door slid up and along the ceiling of the garage, and Gayle drove out of the downpour into the dry safety of the four-car unit.

Stepping out of the car, she turned and ran a caressing gaze over the three other vehicles parked in neat alignment, a sigh whispering through her lips as her glance came to rest on the middle car, a gleaming Rolls Royce Silver Cloud. The Rolls had been Louis's third love. The house had been his second most prized possession. Gayle had been his first passion.

Catching her lower lip between her teeth to prevent a moan of protest against fate, Gayle turned sharply and rushed to the side door, which led to the house through the laundry room.

You're just tired, she assured herself, blinking away the tears gathering in her eyes. A cup of hot tea and some food will chase the depression. Gayle had been making herself the same promise every day since she'd returned to her law practice five months before.

"Good evening, Mrs. d'Acier." Marge Benton, Gayle's housekeeper, greeted her warmly as Gayle entered the kitchen. "I have a pot of tea on and muffins baking for you." Catching sight of Gayle's soaked raincoat and soggy shoes, Marge urged, "But you'd better change first before you catch your death."

Agreeing with Marge and greeting her in the same breath, Gayle walked out of the kitchen and along the short hall to the shallow flight of four steps that led to the master bedroom. A small smile played at the corners of her mouth. Did anybody really ever *catch* their death from being wet? she wondered in amusement. Gayle very seriously doubted it.

Entering the bedroom, Gayle paused, the smile fading. Would she ever be able to walk into this room without expecting to see Louis sitting in his chair in front of the wide window that looked out over the garden at the side of the house? Gayle very seriously doubted that as well.

Her lips now slanted in curved lines of sadness,

Gayle slid out of her wet shoes and raincoat and deposited them both in the connecting bathroom to dry. After peeling off her pantyhose, she slipped into soft ballerina-style slippers, then left the room to return to the kitchen. Despite Gayle's soft house shoes, Marge heard her approach. She was pouring tea into a delicate platinum-rimmed cup when Gayle entered the room.

"There's your mail and phone messages." Marge nodded at the neat pile beside the woven place mat on the butcher-block tabletop. "There'll be more than enough food if you want to have guests for dinner."

Guests for dinner? Gayle frowned. What in the world was Marge talking about? she wondered, seating herself. She rarely had guests for dinner. Gayle's confusion vanished with the reading of the first phone message. The neatly penned message was brief and to the point: *Brant called. He has a party very interested in the house. Are you free for dinner to discuss it?*

Marge's earlier reference to the note was an indication of her relationship with Gayle. A fifty-two-year-old spinster, Marge had adopted Gayle months before Louis had brought her to the house as his bride. Marge never hesitated at poking her rather long nose into Gayle's business, especially since Louis's death. Gayle wouldn't have had it any other way.

"What time did Brant call?" Gayle asked, lifting the cup to her lips. More than a friend, Brant was Louis's only child, and Gayle's best friend's husband.

"Shortly after noon."

"Did you inquire about Charley?"

In the process of sliding a tray of muffins from the

oven, Marge paused to give Gayle a wry look. "Of course I inquired," she scolded gently. "Charley is fine." A twinkle lit her eyes from within. "Brant said she's as round as a barrel and loving every minute of it."

Gayle laughed softly. Who would ever have believed that the very elegant, ultraslim Charlott d'Acier—nee Marks—who was also Max Charles, the famous artist, would revel in being pregnant? And with her second child at that!

"Charley must really be slurping the milk shakes this time," Gayle observed, "and she still has five months to go." Gayle shook her head, remembering Charley's consuming passion for strawberry milk shakes during her first pregnancy two years earlier.

"This time it's macaroni salad," Marge informed her dryly.

"Macaroni salad!" Gayle exclaimed in a burst of laughter. "Good heavens! Charley never even *liked* macaroni salad."

"Being pregnant does seem to have a strange effect on some women's appetites," Marge observed sagely —as if from firsthand experience, of which she had none.

"Hmmm." Gayle hid her expression behind the cup as she sipped at her tea. There was little point in displaying the sudden pain she felt, yet she could not prevent the twist that pulled at her lips. Gayle had wanted desperately to have Louis's child, but it was simply not meant to be. How she would have loved experiencing pregnancy's strange effects.

Slowly chewing a small bite of a blueberry muffin,

Gayle hid her dulled eyes from Marge by going through her messages and mail. There was the usual once-a-month duty call from her mother, who, Gayle knew, didn't really give a damn. That fact no longer had the power to hurt Gayle. There was a reminder call from her dentist: it was time for her six-month checkup. There was the usual assortment of junk mail. All of it mundane, none of it of any interest to Gayle. Except the message from Brant. That call she'd return as soon as she'd finished her snack.

As Gayle popped the last bit of muffin into her mouth, Marge filled her cup with fresh tea. Smiling her thanks, Gayle carried it with her into the study and to Louis's wide desk. After dialing Brant's home number, she sipped at her tea and stared at the painting on the wall above the stone fireplace. The painting of a modern-day Madonna was riveting, and one of Charley's best works. Thinking of Charley brought a smile to Gayle's somber face.

"Hello." The happy sound of the artist's voice deepened Gayle's smile.

"Hello yourself," Gayle responded. "How are you feeling?"

"Fat and happy," Charley laughed. "More to the point, how are you?" she asked with instant concern.

"I'm fine, Charley, really. I wish you and Brant wouldn't worry about me so much."

"Gayle, Brant and I both love you!" Charley sighed. "How could we help but worry?"

"But I really am fine." Gayle infused her tone with a confidence she was far from feeling. "Going back to work has helped enormously," she lied. Going back to work merely kept her mind occupied from nine to six. "Marge tells me Brant called," she went on, in an attempt to change the subject.

"Yes. An old friend of his has just moved back to Philadelphia after being away for some years, and he's looking for a house, price no object." Charley paused for breath before continuing. "Brant would like to discuss it with you."

"All right." Even as she agreed, Gayle winced again. It would be hard leaving the house and its memories, even if she knew she had to for her own peace of mind. "Why don't you and Brant join me for dinner? Marge assures me there's more than enough."

There was a short moment of silence. Then Charley asked softly, "Would you mind if we brought Brant's friend along?"

"No." Gayle paused to draw a deep breath. "I'll give him the guided tour. We'll eat at eight, but come early for pre-dinner drinks."

After she hung up the phone, Gayle sat staring through the dark window at the even darker shape of the large elm tree beyond the pane.

I must do it, Louis, she thought, sending the words out beseechingly. I don't want to, but I must.

Closing her eyes briefly against the sudden hot sting of tears, Gayle pushed the chair away from the desk and stood up. She had begun talking to Louis, inside her mind, several months ago. It had to stop. The house had to go.

Gayle was not at all worried about meeting Brant's friend. Though she had always been retiring by nature, Gayle had learned to present herself to the world as a composed, confident lawyer. Only those who knew her well, close friends like Charley and Brant, knew that a very shy thirty-three year-old woman hid behind the facade.

Thus, expecting an evening of good conversation and needed relaxation, Gayle was not at all nervous. Not until she opened the door to her guests a few minutes after seven-thirty.

Brant was as he always had been—tall, attractive, urbane. Charley was even more beautiful than she ever had been, glowing with impending motherhood. Brant's friend was an altogether different proposition.

The man Brant ushered into Gayle's foyer had the words "street moxie" stamped on him like a fashion designer's label. Within seconds, Gayle's eyes had categorized and impressed his features onto her mind.

He stood every bit as high as Brant's six foot plus; his shoulders were every bit as wide. There the similarity between the two men ended. In comparison to Brant's muscular slimness, this man appeared whipcord lean and rangy. In contrast to Brant's aristocratically delineated features, this man's rugged face looked as though it had been harshly molded in tempered steel. His eyes, a startling cold sea-green, were a shock to the nervous system. Gayle was at once repelled and fascinated.

"Gayle, I'd like you to meet an old friend of mine," Brant said easily as he closed the door, giving Gayle a second's panicky sensation of being trapped. "Jacob Munger"—a teasing smile twitched Brant's lips—"my stepmother, Gayle d'Acier."

The sea-green eyes clouded and reddish-brown brows inched up imperceptibly as Jacob swept Gayle's body with an all-encompassing glance.

"*This* is your stepmother?" Jacob Munger's voice, smooth and rich as dark chocolate, gave another jolt to Gayle's nerves.

Before Gayle could respond, before she could think of a *way* to respond, Charley laughed softly.

"Oh, Jake! I know it was unfair of us to leave you in the dark about Gayle, but it wasn't deliberate, honestly," she assured him. "And your expression is priceless."

"Nothing's priceless."

A chill permeated Gayle's body. This hard-faced man was not trying to be humorous. He was dead serious! This Jacob Munger was firmly convinced that everything, and probably everybody, had a price. Her eyes widening slightly in a combination of wonder and horror, Gayle tried to imagine where Brant had ever met this cynical person.

"But I forget my manners." His lips curving into a parody of a smile, Jacob extended a long, bony-fingered hand. "Mrs. d'Acier, it is an enlightenment to meet you."

A warning, a premonition, *something* sent an alarm ringing shrilly through Gayle's entire being. Fighting a sensation unbelievably like actual fear, she had to force herself to place her hand in his. Brief as it was, the physical contact ignited a spark that seemed to set her arm on fire.

"Mr. Munger." The tremor in her voice betrayed the fear, at least to Jacob Munger. For although neither Charley nor Brant appeared to notice, Jacob's lids narrowed over eyes suddenly glittering with inner amusement.

"Please, call me Jake"—his pause was barely discernible—"Gayle."

A flash of intense anger brought Gayle to a realization of time and place, and the fact that *she* was the hostess here, and *he* the guest. Drawing upon years of acquired composure, Gayle indicated the sunken living room with a carefully casual movement of her hand.

"But I forget *my* manners," she said gently, imitating his earlier mockery. "Come in, please." Leading the way down the two flagstone steps into the room, Gayle felt a curl of satisfaction as she swept her gaze over its generous proportions.

"Very nice."

Gayle's glow of pride dimmed in the light of Jake's approval. For a moment she had forgotten the reason for his presence in her home. Her spine stiffening with resistance, she watched him as he appraised the room with his cool eyes.

"Thank you." Gayle's automatic response was forced through a throat suddenly dry with apprehension. Instinct told her that from Jake Munger "very nice" was tantamount to an effusive "I love it" from anybody else, and she didn't want him to love it!

Baffled by her conflicting emotions, Gayle murmured a distracted "if you don't mind" to Brant's offer to fix the drinks. Then she joined Charley in light before-dinner conversation without having the vaguest idea of what they were discussing. On the surface she was her normal unruffled self, but inside she was a jumbled mass of confusion.

This is ridiculous! she chastised herself. Do you or do you not want to sell this house? I do, Gayle decided firmly, then undermined her own position by amending, but not to this man!

". . . and wait till you see the study!"

Charley's enthusiastic remark drew Gayle's complete attention. Though she didn't even remember having accepted a drink from Brant, Gayle came to the realization that she had swallowed over half of the wine in the glass she was clutching. While she sat in a daze, the conversation had progressed, unheard by her.

"I was hoping for the grand tour before dinner," Jake drawled pointedly. "Is there still time?" Shifting his gaze, he stared directly into Gayle's eyes.

What to do? Floundering, Gayle stared back at him. Then inspiration struck. There really was very little time before dinner. In fact, just enough time for the quickest grand tour ever! Controlling the urge to jump to her feet, she rose with studied grace, a pleased smile curving her soft lips.

"Of course." Regally sailing by him, she led the way out of the room and along the hall to Louis's— she would *always* think of it as Louis's—study. Inviting Jake inside with a casual sweep of her hand, Gayle spoke in a monotone.

"This is the study Charley couldn't wait for you to see." Though Gayle caught the sharp look Jake turned on her, she continued levelly. "Has Brant informed you of my plan to sell the furnishings along with the house?" His face somber, Jake nodded briefly. His eyes asked why. Gayle chose to ignore the query. Why bother to explain to this man that selling the house while retaining the furniture would defeat her purpose? The most important mementos of her life with Louis could be stored in her heart.

"With the exception of the Max Charles." A fleeting smile shadowed her lips as she followed the direction of his glance to the painting on the far wall. "That, of course, is not for sale."

"Beautiful," Jake murmured as if to himself. Then, turning back to her again, he said, "I don't blame you for not wanting to part with it. It is absolutely beautiful."

The deep timbre of Jake's voice affected Gayle strangely. Would his voice hold that tremor of near adoration when he complimented a woman? The thought shocked Gayle into startled awareness. What was wrong with her this evening? She didn't care a snap how Jake sounded while murmuring endearments to a woman! Still . . . In a frantic attempt to avoid her own thoughts, Gayle rushed into speech.

"Yes," she agreed. "But then, I consider all of Charley's work exceptional."

"Hmmm . . ." Jake regarded her through eyes that revealed nothing of what he was thinking. "There are several *exceptional* pieces in this room." While offering the opinion, Jake slowly ran his gaze the length of her body and back, his eyes colliding with hers at the end of his perusal.

Pieces? Pieces! Gayle felt her cheeks grow hot and

her hands grow cold simultaneously. Her spine stiffening with offense, she spun around to stalk out of the room and immediately banged her shin on the corner of the leather-covered club chair in front of the desk.

Biting back a cry of pain, Gayle reached for the chair back to steady herself and felt her hand grasped by long, bony fingers.

"Are you hurt badly?" Jake's quiet voice sounded beside Gayle's ear. His warm breath caressed her skin. His hard fingers played havoc with her senses.

"No! No, really, I—oh!" Gayle's attempt at coherence collapsed as Jake claimed her waist with his other hand. As his arm tightened, Gayle's resistance fell apart.

Sighing, she leaned back against the firm support of his chest, appreciatively breathing in the sharp, tangy scent of after-shave and pure maleness. For the moment she felt cosseted, and comforted, and cared for. And for the moment she was content to drift with the sheer pleasure of once again being held close to a man.

"Your hair smells like lilacs."

The darkly exciting sound of Jake's voice sent a shudder of awareness through Gayle's body, awakening her to a need she'd thought entombed with Louis. The brush of his lips against her temple increased the need to a pulsating demand. She knew she had to move away, yet she could not. She knew she should protest, yet the words would not come.

Hating the weakness that rendered her pliant, Gayle caught her lower lip between her teeth as Jake slowly turned her around into his embrace. The feeling of her breasts being carefully crushed to his chest was shattering. Mindlessly, Gayle lifted her arms and curled them around his strong neck, shivering in response as his mouth trailed from her temple to her throat. Closing her eyes, she let her head fall back in invitation.

Slowly, their touch feather-light, Jake's parted lips explored the silkiness of her arched neck, eliciting a ragged moan when the tip of his tongue touched her wildly beating pulse.

"You taste like lilacs, all sweet and dewy fresh," he groaned against her skin. "I want to taste all of you. Come to bed with me."

It was not Jake's outrageous suggestion that brought Gayle to her senses, but the intense desire she felt to say yes. Sliding her hands down the front of his silk-shirted chest, she pressed lightly in a silent plea for release. Positive Jake would pursue his advantage, Gayle was surprised when he loosened his hold and stepped back.

"Are you all right?" he demanded softly.

Unsure if he referred to her bumped shin or her emotional condition, Gayle felt it prudent to encompass both with a simple nod of her head.

"Then, shall we continue with the tour?" His green eyes shimmered, and Gayle wondered whether his expression was one of desire or amusement.

Glancing at the clock on the mantel, she shook her head. "It's too late. My housekeeper will be announcing dinner any second. We'd better return to the living room, and Brant and Charley." And safety, she added silently.

"As you wish." Releasing her fully, Jake motioned for her to precede him out of the room. As she stepped by him, he whispered, "I can wait."

Gayle's step almost faltered. Had Jake meant he could wait for the tour of the house or for the suggested tour of her? Glancing at him sharply, Gayle read his meaning clearly in the sensuous curve of his lips. Doubly wary of him now, she quickened her step. Jake's knowing laughter followed her into the living room.

"Well, Jake, what do you think of the house?" Brant asked as Jake strolled into the room at a leisurely pace behind Gayle. "It's a beauty, isn't it?"

"Actually, we got no farther than the study," Jake replied dryly, accepting a fresh drink from Charley. "But your lovely wife was correct." Lifting his glass, Jake saluted Charley. "I was enthralled in the study."

Gayle went warm all over. Trying to ascertain if Brant and Charley had picked up Jake's odd phrasing, she glanced quickly from one to the other, sighing with relief when it appeared obvious they had not. Barely attentive to the ongoing discussion about the time and care Louis had put into furnishing the study, Gayle scrutinized her guest more closely, once again wondering where Brant could have met the man.

In the subdued hall lighting, Jake's hair had appeared dark brown in color. Now, as he stood almost directly in the glow of a floor lamp, Gayle could see that his hair was really more of a russet shade. It was rather startling in contrast to those chilling sea-green eyes. His clothes were casual but noticeably expensive, hand-tailored if Gayle was any judge at all. His jacket was of a fine Harris tweed, his perfectly fitting slacks in a matching shade of brown. His shirt was pale blue, and silk—Gayle imagined she could still feel the texture of the material against her fingertips. But it was his shoes that were the most impressive. They were of the finest leather, and obviously handmade.

Intent on her examination of him, Gayle was oblivious to the fact that Jake's shuttered eyes were watching her, too. His cool observation both startled and embarrassed her when he asked softly, "You have a question, Gayle?"

Caught staring rudely, Gayle raked her mind for a plausible query. Brant unknowingly came to her rescue simply by looking at her expectantly.

"I . . . uh, couldn't help wondering where you and Brant met." As soon as the words were out, Gayle felt like a fool. The question sounded snobbish, even to her own ears. The smile that slanted crookedly across Jake's lips affirmed her fear that he'd caught the note of condescension.

"We met in college." Brant offered the information. "We became instant friends when we discovered each other's passion for philosophy." Brant chuckled. "I might add that we were in the minority."

Philosophy? Gayle stared at Brant in sheer disbelief. She had no trouble at all believing that Brant had been interested in philosophy, but Jake Munger!

Gayle could better see Jake disrupting the precepts of ethics, rather than studying them. In her mind, Jake had the look of a predator, not a scholar.

"What baffles you, Gayle?" Jake probed wryly. "The fact that Brant and I are friends? Or that our friendship was forged in Philosophy 101?"

Feeling transparent, Gayle laughed self-consciously. "The philosophy, I suppose," she lied. "Brant has always appeared such a physical person to me . . ." Gayle let her voice trail off. Where could she go from there without compounding her own foolishness? Fortunately, Marge announced dinner before either Jake or Brant could pursue the topic.

As Jake offered his arm to Charley to escort her to the dining room, Brant grinned at Gayle and did likewise. "Physical, am I?" he teased as they entered the spacious room. "Has my lovely wife been extolling my prowess?"

From anyone else, the question would have sent a wave of scarlet to Gayle's cheeks. From the irrepressible Brant, the query was almost expected.

"Well, actually no," Gayle murmured primly, then taunted, "and, by her silence, I was convinced you possessed none."

Brant's laughter filled the room with a delightful sound, and Gayle's heart with aching loneliness. She could hear Louis in Brant's laughter, could almost relive again the many times she and Louis had exchanged banter of this kind with Brant and Charley. Denying the need to cry, Gayle forced a smile to her stiff lips. She had betrayed one type of emotion to

Brant's hard-faced friend; she'd as soon die as betray the grief she still endured.

"As you can see, Jake"—Gayle nearly choked on his name—"this is the dining room." Completely unaware that her tone had taken on a wistful note, she continued. "My husband decorated it himself."

Her glance swept over the miniature-patterned wallpaper, the antique satin drapes, and the rich patina of the Duncan Phyfe furniture. Visually caressing the room, she was oblivious to the look that passed among her three guests. The first indication she had that every nuance of regret she was feeling was being observed came with Brant's gentle comment.

"You love this house, Gayle." As he pulled her chair out for her, he arched one brow. "Are you positive you want to sell it?"

"I must." Gayle hadn't intended to be quite so blunt, or so revealing. Managing a shaky laugh, she seated herself at the table. "It's much too large for me, and now that I'm a working woman again I really don't have the time to give it the attention it needs."

"What it needs is children."

Gayle had to clamp her teeth together to keep from gasping at the cruelty of Jake Munger's remark. Had his taunt been issued deliberately? Had Brant told Jake of her disappointment in not being able to conceive a child with Louis? Gayle mentally rejected that idea. Surely, not even this indifferent man would deliberately rub verbal salt on an emotional wound. Would he? Gayle decided to find out.

"I don't know if Brant has mentioned it, Jake, but I

have no children." Gayle kept her voice steady with effort.

"No, he hasn't." Jake stared straight into Gayle's eyes. "But I assumed as much. On the other hand, I *do* have children"—his hesitation was barely noticeable—"but no wife."

Chapter Two

She's perfect. Savoring a sip of his after-dinner liqueur, Jake minutely examined the softly rounded curves of his hostess. Well, he amended, not quite perfect, perhaps, but close enough for his purposes.

At the moment, she was involved in an animated discussion with Brant and Charley, and she was sparklingly alive. Sipping again from the tiny glass, Jake swallowed a smile along with the fiery Drambuie. Gayle's face was animated, yes, but not as interestingly animated as it had been earlier in the study. Then her features had been alive with sexual awareness—awareness of him.

Carefully keeping his own expression impassive, Jake scrutinized the woman he'd set his sights on just moments ago.

About nine or ten years younger than his own thirty-nine, Jake judged, even though she looked still younger. Having held her in his arms, he knew she stood a good ten inches shorter than his six foot two, but height hadn't been one of his major considerations anyway. A little too well padded, perhaps, but—Jake shrugged mentally—it would certainly be a change from the usual "clothes rack" type he'd become used to. Besides, he'd rather enjoyed the feeling of that abundantly soft flesh against his palms.

Tipping his glass, Jake finished his drink, then leaned forward to place the glass on the oval tray on the coffee table. As he sat back again, his breath caught in his throat when Gayle laughed softly at something one of the others said.

The sound of Gayle's laughter was as gentle as everything else about her seemed to be. Her voice was gentle. Her movements were gentle. The curves of her cheekbone and lipline were gentle. Her dark brown eyes were gentle. And, incredibly, even the wave in her light brown hair looked gentle. Though her face was not beautiful, it was lovely in a—Jake smiled in self-derision—in a gentle way.

Quietly observing her, Jake realized the attraction he felt for her stemmed from the very differences between Gayle and the women he'd been involved with during the last few years. Every one of those women had been tall, and slender, and about as gentle as an Amazon. As playmates they had suited Jake's requirements well. But now Jake was no longer playing. The spasm of pain that had washed over

Gayle's face when he'd observed that what the house needed was children had told him much about her unfulfillment.

His eyes darkening with intent, Jake made a firm decision. Yes, Gayle d'Acier would fit into his plans very nicely.

Becoming uncomfortable, Gayle shifted unobtrusively in her chair. Why was Jake Munger trying to stare holes through her? The reason that sprang to mind sent a wave of warmth to her face that Gayle prayed would be attributed to the heat from the fire crackling in the fireplace.

Was Jake remembering her response to him in the study, and possibly calculating his chances of a repeat performance? A chill followed the heat wave. What must he think of her? As to that, what was she to think of herself? Never before in her life had she reacted to a man with such wantonly uninhibited fervor! Why, not even with Louis had she . . . Gayle's mind went numb with shock. Good heavens! Was she *that* lonely?

". . . and you're still planning to have Thanksgiving dinner with us, aren't you?"

Gayle dragged her attention away from her disquieting thoughts to concentrate on Charley's question. "Yes, if you still want me," she finally answered.

"Gayle, really!"

"Of course we still want you."

Though Brant and Charley replied in unison, Brant elaborated, "We wouldn't want to break a three-year tradition."

"As Marge is looking forward to spending the day with her brother and sister-in-law," Gayle said quietly, "I'm relieved to hear you say that." A moment later, her relief turned to chagrin as Brant arched a brow at Jake.

"And what about you, Jake? Have you decided whether or not you're going to accept our invitation?"

"Yes, I've decided." Jake smiled slowly. "I'd be delighted to spend the holiday with you."

Gayle still felt the shock of Jake's quiet acceptance long after her guests had departed and the house was wrapped in silence. Curled up in the chair by her bedroom window, she brooded over the evening, and the man who had made a shambles of it—and her. Evasively disregarding her moment of madness in the study, Gayle decided she did not particularly like Jacob Munger.

Who was he? she asked herself repeatedly. And why in heaven's name had Brant invited him to dinner on Thanksgiving? In the three years that she'd been a member of the d'Acier family she had not known anyone but family members to be invited for holiday meals. So, why had Brant broken tradition by inviting Jake? Gayle shook her head in confusion. Obviously, Brant and Jake were much closer friends than she'd believed. Strange, they were so drastically different, too, Brant so polished and urbane, Jake so arrogantly, blatantly hard. Even more surprising was the fact that Charley had apparently made fast friends with Jake also.

Frowning into the darkness beyond the window, Gayle shuddered delicately at the memory of Jake's appraising eyes and cynical smile. How could Charley have accepted him so easily? Why, the man was a barracuda! And, having known Charley for a long time, Gayle was well aware of Charley's contempt for men of the barracuda variety.

Be very careful around this man, she advised herself nervously. Without knowing exactly why, Gayle had the uneasy feeling that this particular barracuda was planning to pick her clean.

"Ridiculous!"

Exclaiming the word aloud, Gayle uncurled her legs and jumped to her feet, telling herself to forget him.

Over four hours later she was still telling herself the same thing. Though now exhausted, Gayle found it impossible to get to sleep with those sea-green eyes mocking her every attempt.

"Come to bed with me."

The groaned plea with its hint of command whispered through Gayle's mind incessantly, sending alternate spurts of heat and cold from her cheeks to the soles of her feet.

Shifting restlessly beneath the now wildly rumpled covers, Gayle raked her fingers through her shoulder-length hair. What was the matter with her? She had never been attracted to Jacob Munger's type. In fact, she had always been wary of *all* men—regardless of type! Louis, her gentle, gallant Louis, had been the very first man she had ever felt at ease with.

"Oh, Louis."

The broken cry sounded harsh in the quiet bedroom. Closing her eyes tightly, Gayle tried to visualize the beloved face. For a second a picture formed, revealing the classically handsome face of Louis d'Acier as he'd looked before the massive coronary that had taken him from her two weeks after his sixty-second birthday. Then the picture dissolved to reform into the rugged, unrelenting lines that made up the ruthless-looking features of Jake Munger.

And that ruthlessness was now centered on her! Gayle didn't know how she knew it, but a sixth sense warned her that Jake had made up his mind to have her. And she was very much afraid that whatever Jake wanted, Jake acquired one way or another.

Shivering, Gayle curled into a ball and tried to deny the sensation of excitement uncoiling in her stomach. After knowing Louis, she could not possibly feel any kind of attraction for Jake! Repeating the words to herself like a prayer, Gayle finally drifted into a restless, dream-fragmented sleep. . . .

The beast was gaining on her. She could feel his hot breath on the back of her neck, could smell the distinctive scent of him, musky, and purely male. Terror closing her throat, she ran faster and faster, and still he gained, drawing ever nearer until, sobbing, she felt a sinewy arm curl around her waist and drag her depleted body against the rock hardness of his. Come to bed with me. Come to bed. Come to . . .

"No!"

A whimper, a moan, but the sound was loud enough to waken Gayle. Swallowing convulsively, she sat rigid in the center of her bed as the dream retreated in the face of the bright fall sunshine streaming through the windows.

Not since she was a teenager had Gayle been

plagued by nightmares. Then there had always been someone or something chasing her too. Gayle had always known that that something was male—a man who would hurt her, hurt her in exactly the same way that other man had tried to hurt her.

Drawing her knees up, Gayle rested her forehead on them as the long-suppressed memory burst through her subconscious.

She'd been thirteen, a very naive thirteen, and the man had been a friend of her mother's. Every time her father was out of town on business, the man had come to their beautiful mainline Philadelphia home. He had always brought her expensive gifts and called her sweetheart, yet there had been something about him that had frightened her. He was very big and muscular, with hard eyes and a raspy voice that Gayle now realized was a result of too much whiskey swallowed neat.

Irene, her exquisitely lovely mother, had patiently explained that the man, whom Gayle knew only as Mark, was very rich and a powerful force in the area. At the time, Gayle's experience of men was limited to her father and the fathers of her friends, all of whom had been born into old money and possessed the graces that accompany it.

Mark was nouveau riche and singularly lacking in all the graces—a fact the young Gayle learned the hard way.

It was a hot July afternoon. Gayle was sunbathing by the pool on the grounds behind the house. Her mother was away, lunching with friends. Except for the live-in housekeeper, who was cleaning closets on the second floor, Gayle was alone. At least she'd thought she was alone until a shadow blocked the sun.

At first, she'd thought a cloud was in the way. Frowning, she opened her eyes, and immediately wished she hadn't. Mark was standing over her, staring, the expression on his face so blatantly lecherous that even in her innocence Gayle could read his intent. Terror closed her throat as his gaze crawled the length of her young body.

"So very slender," he observed in that scary, whiskey-rasped voice. "And so very inviting," he went on, his glance fastening on her small, still forming breasts.

She seemed to be frozen to the air mattress she was lying on. Panic stifled the scream rising to her lips as he dropped to his knees beside her.

"Don't be afraid, little girl," he'd muttered as he lowered his head. "I'm going to teach you to be a woman."

Even when she finally screamed, his lips, wet and hot, muffled the sound, and his hateful, thrusting tongue pushed it back into her throat.

The pain he inflicted with his brutal mouth galvanized her. Gayle began to fight like a wild thing, kicking out at him with her feet, pounding at his shoulders with her small hands, twisting and heaving her body. Her resistance only seemed to inflame him. Shifting his large, muscular frame, he crushed her beneath him, settling himself shockingly between her thighs. When his big hand covered her breast Gayle bit him . . . hard enough to draw blood. All it gained her was more pain.

"Damn you!" he snarled, punishing her by grasping her tender flesh viciously. Once again her scream was silenced by his brutish mouth.

Clamping his lips to hers, he began to tear at the skimpy bottom half of her bikini. Barely able to breathe, Gayle's struggles grew weaker and weaker as gray mist turned to black in her mind.

At the very edge of consciousness she dimly heard his guttural curse, and then she was free. Her eyes tightly closed, she lay, gasping great gulps of air into her oxygen-starved body.

"Cover yourself," he whispered harshly. "Someone's coming."

It was then Gayle heard the car drawing to a halt in the driveway on the other side of the tall hedges that surrounded the pool area. Shaking, gulping back the sobs that choked her, she drew the brightly patterned material over her aching breasts and hips.

"Mark, are you back there?"

Mark caught Gayle's chin in a bruising grip as her mother's voice called from the driveway.

"Yes, I'm by the pool, getting to know Gayle," he called back pleasantly. Then, his tone dropping to a snarl, he warned, "Don't you ever tell anybody about this."

Gayle never did.

The sound of her own ragged breathing brought Gayle out of memory's grip and to the realization that her face was wet. Her tears were not for herself as she was now, but for the innocent she had been at the time of that disgusting incident.

How very happy she'd been in that first year of her

teens—and how very blind. She had practically worshiped her father, and had adored her beautiful mother. Mark, however, had forced her eyes open.

Filled with loathing, she had watched her mother greet him that day. They were all there, all the nuances and telltale signs that she'd been oblivious to before. Her mother and the beast were lovers! What did that make her father?

Gagging on the nausea surging into her throat, Gayle had muttered an excuse. Then, tears streaming down her sun-flushed cheeks, she had run for the house and the solitude of her bedroom.

From that day on, even after Mark had disappeared from the scene to be replaced by a man ten years her mother's junior, Gayle had not been able to look at Irene without feeling a twist of disgust in her midsection. And she had not been able to look at her father without feeling both compassion and scorn.

Up to that day Gayle had argued fiercely against attending the private New England girls' school her mother had chosen for her. After that day she had been relieved to escape the house and her parents.

In time, Gayle had managed to submerge the incident deep within her subconscious. But the emotional ramifications had left her wary of men . . . most particularly very strong, tough men. Louis d'Acier had been neither physically strong nor tough by nature.

A true gentleman, Louis had captured Gayle's interest from the moment she was introduced to him. Discounting the nearly thirty-year age span that separated them, she had decided almost immediately that she wanted to be his wife. The hard part had been convincing Louis! Still a virgin and inexperienced with men, Gayle had sought help in her campaign to corral Louis into marriage.

Sitting now with her chin propped on her knees, Gayle smiled in remembrance of the night she had gone to Charley's apartment seeking advice and had left with an unexpected ally in the person of Louis's own son, Brant. Louis had slipped a diamond-encrusted wedding band onto Gayle's finger less than two months after Brant and Charley had exchanged marriage vows.

"Louis."

Sighing, Gayle lay back against the pillows, unmindful of the time and the fact that she was surely going to be late for work. She had no pressing appointments that morning. All that awaited her in the office was the usual dry paperwork; it would keep for a few hours.

Thoroughly relaxed now that the nightmare had receded, Gayle drifted near the edge of sleep as more recent, pleasant memories flowed gently through her mind. Absently rubbing the diamond ring on her wedding finger, she relived the sweetness of her time with Louis.

What a gentle, caring man Louis had been . . . and what a gentle, caring lover. With infinite patience and tenderness, he had initiated her into the world of love, soothing her fears with gentle words and hands.

How very different Louis had been from the brutish Mark. And how different from Jake Munger.

The thought shook Gayle into full wakefulness. Was that why Jake unnerved her so? Was Jake Munger another Mark? Sinking her teeth into her lower lip, Gayle considered the possibility. Both men were rough-hewn and tough-looking in appearance. Mark had wielded power in the community; Jake had an aura of power about him. Were there other similarities?

Would Jake savage a young girl—or even a mature woman?

No! The denial sprang, fierce and swift, out of nowhere. Stunned into stillness by her mind's vehement rejection of Jake in the role of brute, Gayle blinked in confusion. Where had the certainty come from? The man was a total stranger . . . yet something deep inside Gayle rebelled at the idea of his deliberately hurting anyone. The inner conflict kept her immovable. The sound of Marge's light tap on the bedroom door broke her strange trance.

"Phone call for you, Gayle," Marge called softly. "Will you take it?"

"Yes, of course." The relief washing through Gayle was immediately stemmed by the disturbing voice of her caller.

"Good morning, Gayle. I hope I didn't wake you." Jake Munger's dry tone indicated his indifference one way or the other. "I called your office. Your secretary told me you hadn't come in this morning." Jake's tone altered slightly, taking on a sardonic note that sent heat to Gayle's cheeks and a shiver down her spine. "Did you have a restless night?"

There was a suggestiveness in his voice that made her feel the way she'd felt the evening before when his lips teased the erratic pulse in her throat.

Sliding her palm over the mouthpiece, Gayle drew several deep, calming breaths while she raked her mind for a subtle yet clear rebuttal. Unfortunately, her mind was blank.

"No," she finally lied when the tension humming over the connecting wires became palpable. "As there was very little work on my calendar, I decided to take the morning off." The explanation had a feeble sound, even to Gayle's own ears. Jake's soft rumble of laughter left little doubt that he felt the same.

"And do you also have a bridge for sale?" he asked dryly.

A bridge? Gayle frowned. What the . . . then a light clicked on in her mind and she went hot all over. In so many obscure words, Jake was calling her a liar! How dare he? she thought angrily, dismissing as irrelevant the fact that in truth she was lying. And what right did he have to question her in the first place? None whatever, she decided irately. Anger banished the numbness gripping her mind and her tongue.

"I thought it was a house you were interested in buying," she taunted with innocent sweetness.

Now Jake's laughter was warmer. "And that's the reason for my call," he informed her after a final chuckle. "I'd like to discuss the house. Would you have dinner with *me* tonight?"

Her mind went blank again. Her frown deepening, Gayle sought the wording of a polite but firm refusal.

Obviously anticipating it, Jake added persuasively, "I'm offering to buy you dinner, Gayle. In a public place. Nothing more." He was quiet for a moment, then challenged, "Will you come? Or don't you trust yourself?"

"Don't be ridiculous!" Gayle reacted swiftly. "Of course I trust myself! I'm not a child, Jake."

"I *was* hoping that was the case," he drawled maddeningly. "So, will you have dinner with me?"

She had neatly backed herself into a corner, and she knew it. Sighing at her own ineptitude, Gayle grudgingly agreed to go with him.

"Good. I have appointments till after six. Would eight be convenient for you?"

Do I have a choice? Gayle bit back the question. Instead, she infused a briskness into her tone that equaled his. "Eight will be fine. I'll be ready."

"For anything?"

"Mr. Munger," Gayle began warningly.

"Eight o'clock," Jake inserted before disconnecting abruptly.

Frustrated at having no outlet for her anger, Gayle slammed her receiver onto the cradle. Why had she agreed to have dinner with him? She didn't want to face Jake over a meal. Gayle's lips turned down in a grimace; she really didn't want to face Jake at all.

Disgusted with him and herself, she launched her still tired body from the bed. Positive that if she stayed home she'd fidget away the day worrying about the evening, Gayle decided to go to the office.

Several hours later she was not only sorry she'd come into the office, she was regretting ever taking up the law in the first place. Even though much of her schooling had proved dry and routine, Gayle had assumed, as probably many had before her, that the actual practice of law would be more exciting. It wasn't. At least the type of family law she practiced wasn't. It was sometimes sad, occasionally pathetic. But exciting?

Gayle shook her head over the will she'd been retained to prepare. The elderly woman had come to Gayle distraught over the dispensation of her few belongings. As the woman had no direct descendants, she was concerned about what would eventually happen to her treasured, though meager, possessions.

Sighing softly, Gayle lifted her eyes from the legal pad in her hand to gaze sightlessly out of the single window in her small office.

Would this be her fate in thirty-odd years? Alone and lonely, doling out her possessions to Charley and Brant's children? The image was chilling and Gayle was relieved when a tap on her door scattered her thoughts. An instant later, one of her colleagues strolled into the room.

"Are you very busy, Gayle?"

"No." Shaking her head, Gayle placed the legal pad on her desk and smiled up at the fair-haired man grinning down at her. "What can I do for you, David?"

"Well, you could start by having dinner with me," he began slowly, then added quickly, "and finish by agreeing to marry me."

After a full month of hearing David Beauchamps propose to her regularly once a week, Gayle should have been used to it. She wasn't. Her smile fading, she gazed into David's serious brown eyes. Why couldn't she feel something other than friendship for him? she wondered sadly. At thirty-four, David was considered to be a very good matrimonial catch. The son of a retired judge, he had everything going for him. Besides being an up-and-coming attorney, he had clean-cut, boyish good looks and an athletic physique. Gayle liked David very much, but that was all. She had always known that they could never be more than friends. The hard part was convincing David of that fact.

"I'm afraid the answer must be no to both your invitations," she said gently.

"You won't even have dinner with me?" David asked incredulously.

"I can't have dinner with you," Gayle corrected softly. "I have a date for dinner, David."

David's shocked expression made Gayle want to laugh and cry at the same time. Was he shocked by the fact that she'd *accepted* an invitation from someone other than himself or that she'd *received* one?

"I . . . uh . . . didn't know that you were seeing another man," he stammered.

"I'm not 'seeing' another man," Gayle said tightly. "This is a business dinner."

David's relieved smile sounded an alarm in Gayle's mind. If he was beginning to think possessively about her, and from his attitude he was, it was time to correct him. The decision made, Gayle pushed her chair away from the desk and stood up.

"David," she began quietly, walking around the

desk to place her hand lightly on his arm, "I think we should come to an understanding."

"That's what I've been trying to tell you for a month now." Sliding his arm along her palm, he caught her hand with his. "You know how I feel about you, Gayle." Before she could respond, he lowered his head and brushed her lips with his.

"David, no!"

Disregarding her order, he applied pressure to her lips while sliding his other arm around her waist to draw her body to his. At the physical contact, something seemed to snap in him and his mouth became hard and savage with suppressed hunger.

At first, Gayle was only mildly annoyed. But when David's tongue thrust boldly between her lips, she began to get angry. Beginning to struggle, Gayle brought her free hand up to push against his chest and twisted her head to free her lips from his crushing mouth.

"David! What do you think you're doing?" she gasped.

"What I should have done weeks ago." His voice had a desperate note that actually frightened Gayle. "No, dammit!" Releasing her hand, he grasped her chin to bring her face around to his. "I should have done this years ago," he amended before crushing her mouth again.

With a sensation of unreality, Gayle felt herself being forced down to the desk. As her back settled on the paper-strewn surface, the reality of her situation forcibly struck her. Was David actually planning to take her here, in her own office, on top of her desk?

The intrusive sound of her intercom buzzer was like music to Gayle's ears.

"Mrs. Hastings on line one, Gayle," her secretary Janine announced briskly.

"Oh, hell!" David exclaimed, straightening and moving away from her.

Unequal to the task of dealing with the woman whose will she'd been working on when David had entered her office, Gayle depressed the button on the intercom with a shaky finger.

"Please tell Mrs. Hastings I'm in conference, Janine. I'll get back to her as soon as I'm free." Flipping the button, Gayle slid off the desk and stared coldly at David. "Have you lost your mind?" she demanded icily.

"Look, Gayle, I'm sorry. I . . . I . . ." David shrugged helplessly. "I'm sorry," he repeated softly. "It's just that . . ." His voice trailed away on a sigh. "I want you so badly."

"And that gives you the right to manhandle me?" Gayle's eyes widened with incredulity.

David shook his head distractedly. "I suppose not, but . . ."

"But nothing!" Gayle interrupted cuttingly. "Wanting is never an excuse for taking by force." An image rose in Gayle's mind of another man, a hard-faced man who had wanted to take her by force. She swallowed against the nausea stinging her throat. "If you ever try anything like that again, David, so help me, I'll . . ."

"I won't," David inserted sincerely. "I give you my word that I won't." Walking to her slowly, he took her hand gently. "I never wanted to hurt you, Gayle. Can you forgive me?"

He looked so miserable, Gayle had little choice but to tell him she did. "But," she added warningly, "you had better be on your best behavior from now on." Turning him toward the door, she gave him a gentle shove. "Now get out of here and let me get to work."

Chapter Three

It wasn't until later, after Gayle had spoken to the anxious Mrs. Hastings and assured her that her wishes would be carried out to the letter, that she allowed herself to examine the incident with David.

What in the world had come over David so suddenly? Gayle wondered in amazement. Or *had* it been a sudden, flashing urge? Shifting her gaze to the window, Gayle probed her memory for answers.

David's attitude toward her had always been respectful, even during the few dates they'd had before she met Louis. Though he'd kissed her good night several times, his approach had always been correct and circumspect. So then, what had released the tiger within the pussy cat? Even as she scrutinized every second leading up to his attack, she knew she'd done nothing to warrant it.

Had the beast of unleashed passion been lurking inside all along, crouching to spring at any given moment, with or without provocation? Did every man carry a hungry beast inside himself? Could there come a moment in every man's life when the beast became totally wild and out of control?

Chilled by the frightening implications of her own thoughts, Gayle shivered in the warmth of her small office. Events in her own life appeared to prove out her conjecturing.

First there'd been Mark, not only prepared but eager to savage a young girl. Had the beast gone wild inside him? Then there was Jake, just the evening before, ready to pounce and take full advantage of the situation when she'd been momentarily off balance after striking her leg against the chair. Had the beast growled hungrily inside him? And now, today, there was David, practically flinging her onto the desk, and himself onto her. Had the beast roared inside him?

Gayle's shiver deepened into a shudder as she followed the theory to its conclusion. Did, then, the hungry beast lurk in all men until, reaching the point of starvation, it broke free of the bounds of conscience and convention, ravaging whatever prey happened to be within grasping distance?

"No!"

Gayle was unaware of murmuring the protest aloud, but she was fully conscious of the denial ringing inside her head. If her reasoning was sound, then no woman was ever truly safe with *any* man. Something within Gayle refused to accept that concept. There had to be a saving grace.

Louis.

Gayle sank wearily against the back of her chair. Dear, gentle Louis. Of course, by the time she'd met Louis he was on the brink of his sixtieth birthday. She had no way of knowing if he'd ever lost his reason to the lurking beast, yet she somehow doubted it. Instinct assured Gayle that Louis had always been exactly as she'd found him. And the same instinct told Gayle that Brant, too, had always held the upper hand over the beast.

At least Charley had never made the faintest sound of complaint. Easier in her mind now, Gayle gave way to the smile tugging at the corners of her lips. Of all the attached women she knew, Charley would have been the very last to tolerate the kind of behavior David had displayed earlier. Possessing much more genuine self-confidence than Gayle could ever dream of, Charley would have slashed David to ribbons with the sharp edge of her tongue.

Gayle's smile broadened into a grin at the picture her mind envisioned. Oh, how she wished she could be more like Charley! And not just in temperament, either! With soft laughter, Gayle glanced down at her well endowed figure. How wonderful it must be to be tall and model slim. Even now, blossoming with impending motherhood, Charley had a lissome look that Gayle had not known since her seventeenth year.

Rising with a grace she was innocently unaware of, Gayle walked to the window. Charlott d'Acier was the personification of everything Gayle wished *she* was, yet, strangely, Gayle felt no envy, only love for her.

Thinking of Charley led to thoughts of the night

before, and the prospective buyer she and Brant had so guilelessly brought to Gayle's home.

Gayle's smile disappeared. In her mind she was positive Jake had a tiger clawing at his insides. And she was having dinner with him in a few short hours!

Why had she agreed to go out with him? Gayle quizzed herself nervously. Hadn't she already decided not to sell the property to him? She had. So why, then, had she accepted his invitation?

Swinging away from the window, Gayle strode back and forth in front of her desk. Could she handle him if he made a move on her the way he had the night before? Even as the question was forming, she stopped dead, shaking her head. Her intellect warned that trying to handle Jake Munger would be like stepping into a cage full of hungry lions and tigers.

By the time she got home from work at six-thirty, Gayle felt physically sick with apprehension. In the hour and a half that followed, she picked up the phone at least ten times with the intention of calling Jake and breaking their dinner engagement. And each time she replaced the receiver in actual fear of hearing him roar with rage.

Definitely a mouse, she decided, asking herself the well-worn question, "Are you a woman or . . ." as she left her bedroom at five minutes to eight. The doorbell rang four minutes later.

Swallowing back the lump that insisted on forming in her throat, Gayle smoothed her hands over the soft wool clinging to her hips. Forcing a weak smile to her lips, she pulled the door open.

"Ah, how rare," Jake murmured, raking her body with cool eyes. "A lovely woman who is also prompt."

Ridiculously, shockingly, Gayle felt a thread of excitement uncurl in her stomach at his casual compliment. Did Jake really consider her lovely? Pleasure held her mesmerized for an instant. Then, coming to her senses, she stepped back.

"I'm ready," she said, inviting him in with a wave of her hand. "I have only to get my coat." Turning away, she opened the door to the closet. Slipping the garment from the hanger, she turned back to face him—and froze. Though Gayle had not heard him move, Jake was standing mere inches away from her, his eyes coolly assessing her.

"Allow me." Extracting the coat from her numb fingers, Jake proceeded to help her into it, a blatantly sensual smile playing on his lips. "That's a beautiful dress," he said softly, then ruined the effect of his compliment by asking, "Did you wear it because it matches the color of my eyes?"

Did it . . . really? Before she could control the urge, Gayle glanced down at the sea-green wool, then back up at his now laughing eyes. Good heavens! The dress *did* match his eyes, almost exactly! Surely she hadn't . . . not even subconsciously . . . had she?

Mutely, Gayle stared into those oceanlike depths and felt herself beginning to drown. Oddly, at that instant, she couldn't have cared less. Oblivious to any danger he might represent, she was acutely aware of every nuance about him. His scent, though subtle, was a heady thing, dark and slightly musky. His skin, deeply tanned, was taut over his cheekbones and gleaming with a fresh-shaved sheen. Tiny lines radiating from the corners of his eyes told their own tale. Of what? Much laughter, or long hours spent squinting in the sunlight? And his mouth. Jake's finely chiseled mouth lured. Knowingly, or unknowingly? This time he brought her to her senses.

"We have a reservation."

I have hundreds of reservations, every one about you. As the thought whispered through her mind, Gayle turned to allow him to assist her with the coat, biting her lip to prevent a gasp when his knuckles brushed against her shoulders.

Moving away from him quickly, Gayle walked to the door, a cry of despair echoing in her mind: What was happening to her?

Determinedly avoiding any and all possible answers, she stepped outside, gratefully gulping in the sharp tang of the cold November air. Revitalized, she hurried along the flagstone walk to where his car was parked in the pine tree-shadowed driveway. Less than two feet from the car, Jake halted her headlong flight.

"They'll hold the table for us, Gayle." A thread of amusement laced Jake's voice. "There's really no need to run."

Moving around her now statue-still form, he opened the passenger door with one hand and curled the fingers of the other around her upper arm. "You're as stiff as a drunk on a three-day bender," he observed mildly, flexing his fingers gently. "Are you afraid of me, Gayle?"

Lord, yes! she thought, trying not to shiver.

"Heavens, no!" she scoffed, somehow managing a throaty laugh. "Would you want me to be afraid of you?" she challenged as he handed her into the midnight-blue Lincoln.

Jake didn't reply until he'd circled the car and slid behind the wheel. Then, shifting in the seat to face her, he stared directly into her eyes. "Being able to instill a little fear in your adversary helps . . . at times." His tone was dead serious.

This time Gayle couldn't contain the gasp that burst from her lips. "*Are* we adversaries?"

"Aren't *all* men and women, to one degree or another?" Jake arched one brow in question. "Adversaries in the business world? Adversaries in the home?" His voice went low. "Adversaries in bed?"

Feeling her cheeks grow hot, Gayle blessed the pine trees for their shadowy cover. Did Jake actually expect her to respond to his suggestive remark? Obviously so, for he sat watching her, waiting.

The silence lengthened between them as Gayle raked her mind for a suitable retort. Gayle felt positive that, as far as Jake was concerned, all association with members of the opposite sex was a battle. But her own memories assured her that male-female encounters need not be like that.

"I don't agree," she finally replied. "My husband Louis and I were certainly not adversaries." Deliberately turning away from him to gaze out through the windshield, Gayle felt a twinge of self-satisfaction at the haughty tone she'd contrived; if anyone deserved a put-down, it was one very arrogant Jake Munger!

* * *

If you continue in this vein you are going to blow it, Jake lectured himself silently as he handled the large vehicle with unconscious expertise. Gayle had not spoken a word since she'd introduced her late husband's name into the conversation.

Bringing the big car to a stop at a red light, Jake slanted a quick glance at Gayle and stifled a curse at the sight of her averted profile.

Clumsy fool! he berated himself. You're never going to achieve your goal using those tactics. The light flicked to green and Jake set the car in motion again. This woman is different. Her difference is the very reason you chose her. She's soft and gentle and, at this point, still grieving for a man who was thirty years her senior. A man, moreover, who was also gentle, as you damn well know.

For several moments, Jake contemplated his memories of Louis d'Acier.

He'd met Louis the summer between his junior and senior years at the University of Pennsylvania. Except for a brief visit, Jake had not gone home that summer because he'd signed on to do general labor with a construction crew. Since Brant had signed on with the same outfit, he'd insisted that Jake save his rooming-house rent by staying at the d'Acier home. Though hesitant about accepting, Jake had capitulated when Brant assured him that his father was in favor of Jake's temporary tenancy.

Jake liked and admired Louis from the moment he met him. Sophisticated, urbane, and a true gentleman, Louis epitomized everything Jake longed to be.

When, in one of his infrequent letters, Brant mentioned that Louis had remarried, Jake silently saluted the newlyweds with outrageously expensive champagne while ostensibly toasting his dinner companion of the evening. And then, almost a year ago, when Brant notified him of Louis's death, Jake had felt the loss deeply.

Now Jake had designs on Louis's widow. A woman every bit as classy as Louis had been.

Classy. Yes, this woman had real, honest-to-goodness class.

Jake's glance shifted from the road to the woman beside him. Despite the stiff, very correct way she held herself, Gayle's cheek curved softly.

Watch yourself, Munger, Jake warned himself mutely. Unless you want to find your plans shot clear to hell, proceed with caution. This lady has known the best.

For some incomprehensible reason, thinking of Louis d'Acier in connection with the woman sitting beside him filled Jake with an emotion quite like jealous rage.

Nonsense! Jake chided himself. Neither rage nor jealousy has anything to do with my plans for Gayle d'Acier.

Nevertheless, Jake had an odd, brackish taste in his mouth.

Now he's angry.

Growing more tense by the second, Gayle shifted slightly in the plush seat in an effort to ease the stiffness of the muscles along her spine.

Well, let him be angry! she thought impatiently.

Who the devil did he think he was, anyway, making veiled insinuations to her? With determination tautening her jawline, Gayle assured herself that she could handle Jake.

"This restaurant doesn't offer curb service."

After the lengthy silence between them, Jake's softly drawled observation startled a gasp from Gayle. Blinking out of her introspection, she glanced around in surprise at the realization that the car was no longer moving. But because they were parked facing a dense stand of trees, there was really very little to see. Frowning, Gayle turned to Jake.

"Where are we?"

"Nowhere sinister, I assure you." Jake's tone held a suspicious note of laughter. "The name of the place is The Hungry Lion. And, as I'm beginning to feel like one, I suggest we exit the car and enter the restaurant." He paused, then added very gently, "We are now ten minutes late."

Releasing the door, he pushed it open and stepped outside. Following his example, Gayle stepped out of the car and stood erect as he rounded the back end.

"Tell me you're one of these 'new women' who prefer to open doors, get out of cars, and generally do everything for themselves." Jake's sardonic drawl indicated he really didn't want her to tell him anything of the sort.

Gayle was sorely tempted to act the part of a women's libber, but she decided on the truth instead. "Mr. Munger, I am thirty-three years old," she began with infinite patience, noting the expression of genuine surprise that widened Jake's eyes. "And, although I have no objections whatever to a man's showing me the accepted courtesies, I am completely capable of opening a car door."

"Are you really thirty-three?" Jake's gaze explored her features intently.

"Yes." Positive he'd thought her older, Gayle made the admission flatly, then added, "Didn't you say something about being late for our reservation?"

"Hmmm?" Jake murmured vaguely, still intent on his scrutiny. Then, abruptly he said, "Yes, we are. Come along." Grasping her hand, he led her across the lot to the restaurant's well lit entrance. As his free hand closed on the large, intricately carved brass door handle, he hesitated, again giving her a hard stare. "Huh"—he expelled his breath sharply—"I would have sworn you weren't thirty yet!"

Preceding him into the crimson-carpeted foyer, Gayle was grateful for the subdued lighting, which concealed the flush of pleasure warming her cheeks. How silly, she thought, averting her face as he assisted her with her coat. Why am I all squishy inside because of an offhand compliment? Regardless, at that moment Gayle felt that she would actually enjoy sharing a meal with Jake.

"Ah, Mr. Munger, good evening." The hostess— tall, elegantly slim, and rather exotically attractive— appeared out of nowhere, her white teeth gleaming as she smiled at Jake. Gayle disliked her on sight. "Your table is ready." Bright blue eyes clung to Jake's face. Gayle's dislike settled into disgust. "If you'll follow me, please?" With a sweeping gesture of her long-fingered hand, the woman led them into the large dining room.

Suddenly swamped with impatience, both at the woman's transparent snub of her, and her own prickly reaction, Gayle raised her head regally and trailed after the hostess's undulating form. On reaching their assigned table, Gayle even managed to smile when the hostess finally deigned to acknowledge her existence with a murmured "Enjoy your dinner."

Oblivious to the shrewd sea eyes observing her, Gayle gazed after the slim, retreating figure.

"She's something else, isn't she?"

Jake's cool observation jarred Gayle, and she clamped her teeth together to prevent the passage of a very unladylike retort. Oh, she certainly had to agree, the woman was something else indeed! In fact, it was that very *something* that bothered Gayle. Was *that* the type Jake found interesting? she wondered with an unfamiliar sensation of despair.

"Quite something." Turning to him, Gayle felt a trill of awareness sing along her nerves. Jake was studying her with the same coolly assessing stare he'd subjected her to the night before, only now his eyes held a hint of sensuality. What is he thinking? she wondered, suddenly short of breath. And do I really want to know? Deciding ignorance was the better part of safety, Gayle scoured her mind for a subject of conversation—any subject of conversation.

"Brant told me you have recently moved back to the Philadelphia area." At Jake's brief nod, she plowed on. "From where?"

"California."

Terse as his answer was, it did explain his deep tan. Gayle waited for him to expand, and when it became obvious he wasn't going to, she asked, "You're from Pennsylvania originally?"

"Yes."

Envisioning an entire evening with her chattering like a magpie and Jake responding with monosyllables, Gayle gave up and sat back in her chair. Returning his frank appraisal with a lot more outward composure than she actually felt, she matched him stare for stare. She was about to drop her gaze when the cocktail waiter came to the table and rescued her.

"White wine?" Jake arched a brow at her.

Though she felt gratified that he remembered her preference of wine as a pre-dinner drink, Gayle smiled nicely at the waiter and ordered a piña colada. She was still feeling nettled by Jake's silent stare treatment.

Jake's soft chuckle teased an answering smile from Gayle's lips. At her concession, he sat forward, leaned his arms on the table, and began talking.

"I'm originally from the Pennsylvania Dutch country, about halfway between Lancaster and Lititz." A smile twitched his lips. "I'm a farmer, you know."

"Really?" Gayle didn't know why this bit of information should surprise her, but it did. Of all the people she'd ever met, Jake looked the least likely to be a farmer.

"Well, I was, until I left home for good," he qualified. "But my father and brothers still farm." His look of amusement gave way to a real, unnervingly beautiful smile. "I'm the black sheep of the family."

Completely beguiled, Gayle smiled back. "In what way?"

"I never wanted to be a farmer, and said so, to my mother's dismay."

The waiter appeared, and Jake sat back while he placed coasters and drinks on the table. The moment the waiter walked away, Jake slid his drink toward Gayle and sat forward again.

"That drink looks like a fruit salad in milk," he observed dryly as she took a tentative sip. "Does it taste as sweet as it looks?"

"You've been living in California and you've never tasted a piña colada?" Gayle exclaimed on a choking laugh.

"I never have," he insisted, laughing with her. "I'm a Michter man." Lifting the squat glass filled with amber liquid, Jake silently toasted her. "I practically cut my teeth on this sour mash." His voice lowered. "It's what keeps us farmers tough."

Gayle's smile faded. "And you are tough, aren't you, Jake?"

"Yes, Gayle, I am tough."

It was a fact, simply stated, and all the more unnerving because of the absence of inflection in his tone. Gayle suddenly felt trapped. Thinking him tough was one thing, but having Jake casually admit to it was something else again. For a few moments, she had actually relaxed with him. Gayle suppressed a shiver. How could she have forgotten?

Jake was still leaning forward in his chair, his green eyes opaque, shuttered, his face as free of expression as his tone.

"Toughness bothers you," he murmured, "doesn't it?"

Gayle moistened her dry lips. "Yes."

"Brant's tough," he said flatly. "Yet he obviously doesn't unnerve you."

"Brant is strong!" Gayle retorted. "There's a difference."

"Semantics," Jake pronounced, still in that same inflectionless tone. "Word games."

Perhaps, Gayle thought, but . . . Unable to maintain his steady regard, she sent her glance roving over the room, seeing yet not registering the subdued elegance of the decor, the pristeen white tablecloths, and real silver-edged china. The soft strains of violins and the murmur of muted conversation failed to penetrate her agitated senses.

At any other time, with almost any other man, Gayle would have savored the establishment's refined ambience. Tonight, Gayle was hardly aware of her surroundings, and much too conscious of the man causing all the havoc within her.

As had happened in the car earlier, the tension grew as the silence stretched between them. Gayle started, swallowing a sharp gasp when his hard hand slid over hers.

"Regardless of what I said before, I don't want *you* to be afraid of me, Gayle." Jake spoke with soft urgency, tightening his hold when she tried to slip her hand from under his. "I have no desire to hurt you in any way." He was quiet for a moment, waiting. Then he ordered gently, "Look at me, Gayle."

Gayle moved her head so slowly there was barely a

ripple in her shoulder-length hair. When her gaze finally settled on him, she was surprised to find him staring at her hair in bemusement.

"Not mousy brown at all," he murmured absently, as if to himself. "There are enchanting, dark red sparks hidden in those brown strands." Shifting his gaze, Jake stared deeply into her eyes. "And sparks hidden in the eyes, too." His voice went low. "Are there sparks of life hidden in the woman as well, I wonder?" he mused in a rough velvet voice.

Gayle's heartbeat seemed to come to a complete stop, then increased to an alarming rate. Her breathing grew slow and shallow. In the background the sound of music and murmured conversation receded, leaving Gayle on her own, drowning in the turbulent sea of Jake's compelling eyes.

"Are you ready to order, sir?"

As quietly polite as it was, the waiter's voice shattered the fragile intimacy between them. Gayle was slow to emerge from the trance. Jake, however, was instantly alert.

"Not quite yet," Jake replied hoarsely. "Give us a few more minutes."

"Certainly, sir," the man murmured, silently fading into the shadows.

Shaken by the overwhelming attraction she'd felt for Jake, Gayle hid her flushed face behind the oversized menu. In her rattled state, the abundance of offerings merely confused her, and she sighed with relief when Jake drew her attention from the incomprehensible card.

"Shall I order for you?" he offered. "I've been here before and know their specialties."

"If . . . if you like." Gayle gratefully closed the menu.

"Is there anything you dislike in particular?"

Gayle shook her head slightly. "No. I like most things."

"Really?" Jake's eyes laughed wickedly at her. "We'll see about that."

Gayle knew with certainty that Jake was no longer talking about food.

Chapter Four

One appetite appeased, Jake cupped the bowl of his wineglass and leaned back into the comfort of the cushioned chair. Sipping the California cabernet sauvignon appreciatively, he ran an encompassing glance over the woman seated opposite him.

She was about to take a bite of boeuf bourguignon, and her lips were parted slightly, revealing even, white teeth. Jake watched as her lips closed over the beef. Imagining his bottom lip caught within the moist warmth of her mouth, he went suddenly hot, and very dry.

Tilting the glass now clenched in his hand, Jake took a long swallow of the ruby-red wine, savoring the taste.

Lids narrowing over eyes glittering silver green, Jake fancied he could actually taste the meat Gayle was chewing so very delicately. He fantasized that he could feel those small teeth sinking gently into his lip.

With the erotic vision came a need so great Jake was shocked into absolute stillness for an instant. Powerless against his imagination, he stared helplessly as she raised her glass and sipped at her wine. He ached to experience the sensation of her soft lips sipping at the tip of the tongue he unconsciously slid along his lower lip.

His entire body tightening, Jake gulped the last of his wine.

"Would you like anything else?" Me, for example, he urged mutely.

"Oh, no, thank you." Gayle shook her head. "I couldn't handle another bite."

You could handle me easily any day, bite me too if you felt like it. Jake's hopeful thoughts brought a smile of self-mockery to his lips. "Coffee, at least," he insisted, enjoying the tiny frown of confusion she revealed at his amusement.

"All—all right, coffee." Gayle hesitated a moment, then asked, "Is something funny? Do I have sauce on my chin or something?"

If you did, I would eagerly lick it off for you, Jake told her silently. "No, Gayle, there's no sauce on your chin. And nothing's funny." Somehow he managed to keep from grinning.

Gayle eyed him skeptically. "Then why were you smiling in that . . . that strange way?"

"Was I? I'm sorry," Jake apologized. The only thing that's strange, he thought, is the strength of the desire I feel for you. "I must have been thinking of

something else." You, his thoughts persisted, biting
on my lip, sipping at my tongue, satisfying this sudden
craving I have to feast on you, and have you feast on
me.

The shaft of desire that pierced Jake's body as a
result of his fantasy was breathtaking. His heartbeat
kicked into high gear, pounding in an unfamiliar way.
Good Lord! He hadn't wanted a woman this badly in
more years than he could remember . . . if ever!

The sound of Gayle's chair being pushed back drew
Jake from his pleasurable self-absorption. Automati-
cally getting to his feet, he raised a questioning brow
at her. "Gayle?"

"Ladies room." Gayle smiled. "Makeup repair."

Exactly as it had the night before, Gayle's sponta-
neous smile stole Jake's breath, and he smiled back,
easily, naturally.

Threading her way through the crowded room,
Gayle forced herself to breathe slowly. It was silly,
and rather schoolgirlish, she knew, yet Jake's smile
had set her heart to fluttering wildly. In fact, she had
been experiencing some difficulty in that area most of
the evening!

Inside the elaborately decorated ladies room, Gayle
sank gratefully onto a plush velvet vanity bench,
positive her shaky legs would not carry her another
step. Slipping a slim brush from her purse, she drew it
through her hair once, then paused as her eyes caught
her reflection in the mirror.

As though drawn by a magnet, she leaned closer to
the silvered glass. Were there really red sparks hidden

within the brown strands of her hair? Curious, she leaned closer still. Or sparks in the depths of her eyes?

In the mirrored image Gayle could see only plain brown hair and eyes, but inside, deep inside, she could feel the hot flare from red sparks of renewed life.

Good heavens! Staring starkly at her own widened eyes, Gayle mentally tested the temperature of her emotions and found them near flashpoint. In the most simple terms, she *wanted* Jake Munger!

Gayle closed her eyes slowly and sat back in sudden weariness. A moment later her eyes flew open again, the pupils dilated with shock. Within those brief seconds of darkness, she had envisioned herself in Jake's strong arms, thrilling to caresses from his hard, long-fingered hands, whimpering with passion stirred by his hot, hungry mouth.

No. No. Raising her hand, she pressed the back of her fingers to her mouth. It simply was not possible! She could not, would not, allow herself to feel physical need for a man like Jake. It was base, and degrading, and . . . and . . .

Gayle pressed her hand to her lips to muffle the sob filling her throat. Inside her mind, memories churned. A big, rough-hewn man dropped to his knees beside her.

"Don't be afraid, little girl. I'm going to teach you how to be a woman."

Then the raspy voice was overlapped by a softer, more recent one.

"I don't want you to be afraid of me, Gayle. I have no desire to hurt you in any way."

Jake's tone had been deeply earnest. So why didn't she feel reassured? Because Jake Munger was dangerous, at least to her. Of that she was positive.

"Louis."

Gayle whispered the name aloud, like a prayer, an entreaty for help. Of course, there was no answer. Gayle knew there never would be. She was on her own, alone and afraid. The image staring at her from the mirror blinked as a name flashed into her mind.

Brant! Perhaps Brant could help her!

The flare of hope in her eyes dimmed even as it began to shimmer. Gayle shook her head in rejection of the idea. What could she say to Brant? Jake was Brant's friend. How could she explain this vague sensation of unease? Gayle could well imagine Brant's expression were she to tell him she was convinced that Jake threatened her in some way. Oh, Brant would be concerned, she knew that. But she also felt quite sure his concern would be for her mental state, not his friend's intentions. And, in truth, could she blame him?

Gayle's shoulders drooped. No, Brant's reaction to any accusation she might lodge against Jake would quite naturally be skeptical. In the years they had been friends, Brant had come to know her very well; he knew her attitude toward men. Moreover, what basis *did* she have for complaint?

In actual fact, very little. Jake might have made a few oblique suggestions, but that was hardly grounds for her to run to Charley and Brant begging for protection.

So, she was strictly on her own.

For one terrifying moment, Gayle felt fear claw at her throat, then, squaring her shoulders, she stared directly into her own eyes.

She was no longer a thirteen-year-old child; she was a fully mature woman. She could protect herself from the likes of Jake Munger. Hadn't she controlled the situation with David that very afternoon?

Confidently lifting the brush again, she smoothed her already smooth hair and stood up. As she walked out of the ladies room, she ignored the knowledge of the vast difference between David and Jake Munger.

With the agility and grace of a natural athlete, Jake rose as Gayle approached the table. His eyes narrowed as he ran a swift glance over her.

"Are you all right?" he murmured, holding her chair for her.

"Yes, of course." Gayle felt a thrill of pride at the cool tone she'd contrived. At least she told herself the thrill was caused by pride, and not the brush of his knuckles along her spine. "Why?"

"You were gone so long, I'm afraid your coffee has gotten cold."

As he went back to his seat, Gayle glanced at the cup in front of him; it was empty. Had she really been gone *that* long? Jake inadvertently answered her silent query.

"I was also beginning to fear you had slipped out the back door or something." Then, as Gayle lifted the fragile cup to her lips, he added, "Don't drink that. I've ordered you a fresh cup."

Gayle had no sooner replaced the cup in its saucer than the waiter appeared, whisking the china off the table as if it had offended him and placing another cup before her. Gayle wasn't sure if she should feel amused or appalled.

When she glanced back up at Jake, his eyes were bright with amusement. The laughter escaped him the moment the waiter was out of hearing.

"Do you suppose there's some sinister person hidden in the shadows cracking the whip at the hired help?" he asked conspiratorially.

"You mean, someone in leather and chains, and all that?" she whispered with a grin.

"At these prices? Hardly," Jake drawled, his lips twitching. "Nothing less than a black tuxedo—with a discreet bulge near the waist—would do for this type of establishment."

Shared laughter eased the tension between them. But it came crackling back the moment they stepped outside. The night air had turned sharp, and as they walked to the car, Jake curled his arm around her shoulders and drew her close to the solid warmth of his body.

"I should have had you wait in the foyer a few minutes while I warmed the car." Jake's breath formed a cloud of mist that caressed her cheek and sent a chill down her spine.

"It's . . . ah . . . no, I'm fine!" To her dismay, Gayle heard the slight rise in her voice as Jake's lips feathered the outer curl of her ear.

"Yes, you are." He whispered directly into her ear,

his breath steamy hot against Gayle's skin. "Fine . . . and extraordinarily innocent for a woman in her thirties."

Gayle didn't respond until after they were both seated inside the car; then she turned to him with a frown.

"Innocent?" Her brows arched. "Jake, I was a wife for two and a half years. And, as you say, I am in my thirties. How could I possibly still be innocent?"

"Point taken," Jake conceded. "All right, if not innocent, then somewhat naive."

"In what way?" she demanded.

"Why are you getting so uptight?" he countered.

"I am not uptight!" Gayle denied hotly.

"Then why are you shouting at me?"

Gayle opened her mouth to dispute him, then closed it again. Her voice had gone up another octave. Darn him! What was he trying to do? Drawing a calming breath, she glared at him; by not doing a thing, he was succeeding!

"If you are quite through with whatever game you are playing," she said softly, succinctly, "I would like to go home now."

"Oh, I'm not playing games, Gayle." Jake's too-soft voice set her nerve ends to quivering. "I think you'll eventually find that I never play games . . . except with my children." One dark eyebrow rose. "Would you prefer that I treat you like a child?"

"I prefer to be taken home," Gayle replied with quiet dignity. "Now. If you don't mind?"

The drive back to Gayle's home was made in the

exact same tense silence as the drive to the restaurant had been. It was not until Jake was escorting her to the door that Gayle realized they had not discussed the house once during dinner, and that had been the reason she'd agreed to go out with him in the first place.

"Are you going to invite me in?" Jake asked as she turned the key and pushed the door open. "For a cup of coffee, or to hear what I've decided about the house?" he added, letting her know he was well aware of the fact that they had not yet even touched on the subject.

Gayle would have sooner faced a cage full of enraged wildcats than Jake Munger, but she said none too graciously, "Yes, of course, come on in."

The moment the coats were hung up, Gayle led the way into the sunken living room, indicated that Jake should have a seat, and then asked quietly, "Well?"

"Coffee?" Jake responded hopefully. "It is cold out there tonight."

Suspicious of the note of entreaty in his tone, Gayle searched his face for a trace of humor. Finding none, she sighed.

"It will only take a moment." Gayle walked to the doorway, then added belatedly, "Make yourself comfortable."

But not too comfortable, she added mutely, pushing through the swing door into the kitchen. As always, Marge had left the room in spotless condition, and Gayle was hesitant to disturb things.

After assembling the automatic coffee maker, Gayle removed cups and saucers from the cabinet.

Quiet as she tried to be, Marge heard her and came out of her small apartment off the kitchen.

"Why didn't you call me?" The older woman frowned her concern. "I'd have done that for you."

"I'm making coffee, Marge, not preparing a seven-course meal." Gayle's smile robbed the gibe of any sting. "I didn't want to disturb you."

"What's to disturb?" Marge smiled back wryly. "The movie I'm watching on TV is so bad, I'm enjoying the commercial breaks more than the story." Her eyes gleamed with interest. "Can I assume the coffee is for Mr. Munger?"

"Yes."

"Well, then," Marge said briskly, "you get back in there and entertain him. I'll take care of the coffee tray." Even as she spoke she was nudging Gayle toward the door.

Entertain Jake Munger? Marge had to be joking! Smiling ruefully, Gayle allowed herself to be evicted from her own kitchen. She paused on the other side of the swing door, drew a deep breath, and squashed the urge to run to her room and lock herself in . . . or was it lock Jake out?

When she reentered the living room, Gayle came to an abrupt halt, eyes narrowing as she viewed the lounging form of her unwelcome guest. Jake had certainly taken her invitation literally! Sprawled lazily on the flower-splashed sofa, he looked comfortable to the point of unconsciousness. Only the glitter of his eyes betrayed his alertness.

"Come sit by me." Jake patted the cushion next to him.

"Ah . . . Marge will be serving the coffee in a moment." Gayle determinedly headed for the matching chair opposite the sofa.

Jake's gaze was directed to the ceiling as if in supplication. "This is a beautiful house."

"Yes." Perhaps he hadn't been seeking guidance, but merely admiring the cathedral ceiling. "Louis designed it." Her pride in her late husband's talent was evident in her tone. Gayle was confused when Jake frowned.

"I know." The sigh that whispered through Jake's lips held a thread of weariness, confusing Gayle even more. "I'm not going to buy your house, Gayle," he added bluntly.

"Why?" Gayle was shocked at the sharp sound of her voice; she hadn't *wanted* him to make an offer on the house—had she?

"I could say it's because I don't like furniture patterned with flowers, but I suppose you wouldn't buy that. Would you?" His gaze dropped from the ceiling to focus on her.

"Flowers?" Gayle shook her head, as if to clear it. "What? Jake, I haven't the foggiest idea of what you're talking about."

"Flowers do suit you," he muttered.

Unsure if she'd heard him correctly, Gayle frowned her perplexity. "I'm sorry. I'm not quite sure I understand." She raised her hands in a little, helpless gesture. "Would you repeat that, please?"

"No." Jake slid his body upright. "I've decided to look for a more rural property, farther out of the city. A place where children can run and play with at least a measure of safety." His sharp gaze took in the fact that Gayle winced at the mention of children. "As beautiful as this place is"—his hand moved in a wave that encompassed the grounds as well as the actual structure—"the highway is really not all that far a—" He broke off, getting lithely to his feet as Marge entered the room carrying a laden tray.

"Here, let me take that." With a few long strides Jake was across the room, relieving Marge of her burden. "The coffee smells delicious."

"Well, if it tastes good, you can compliment Gayle," Marge said dryly. "She made it. But, if you like the pound cake"—she nodded at the generous slices of buttery-looking cake arranged neatly on a gilt-edged plate—"you can save your praises for me." Tossing a grin over her shoulder, Marge headed for the door. "*I* whipped that up this afternoon."

Jake chuckled appreciatively. "I like that lady's style," he said with a laugh, placing the tray on the low, kidney-shaped table between the sofa and the chair Gayle was sitting on. "Cream, no sugar, right?" he asked even as he poured a slender stream of cream into one of the cups.

Wondering at the ease with which he'd reversed their roles, Gayle accepted a cup of coffee and a small dessert plate from him with a murmured "thank you."

Settling the plate on her lap, she sipped at the aromatic brew while studying him over the rim of the cup. At his ease as he rested against the plush sofa back, Jake appeared deceptively mellow—and dangerously attractive.

A thrill uncomfortably like sensuous pleasure

wound its way through Gayle's midsection as she covertly observed him consuming the rich cake. The simple act of chewing riveted her gaze to his sharply delineated jawline. Jake raised his cup to his mouth, drawing Gayle's gaze with it. The male lips that lightly touched the cup's rim were thin and hard-looking, but amazingly, beautifully sculpted.

The thrill intensified as Gayle imagined those hard lips drinking thirstily from hers. Hastily averting her eyes, she found her gaze skimming over the chiseled planes of his face, noting a tiny scar at the outer edge of one boldly outlined cheekbone.

How had he acquired the scar? Gayle's imagination took flight as she speculated. A fall from a tree when he was a boy? A football injury in high school or college? A brawl in a bar during his younger, more impetuous days? The last possibility she discounted immediately, for no other reason than the certainty that if Jake had been involved in a barroom brawl he would have inflicted wounds, not received them. Strangely, the mental image of Jake holding his own in a free-for-all, knock-down-drag-out fight brought a smile to Gayle's lips.

"Pleasant thoughts?"

Gayle blinked in confusion. "I beg your pardon?" Startled out of contemplation, she found her gaze captured by a sea-green stare.

"You were obviously light years away, and you were smiling." Jake's tone was frosty. "I asked if your thoughts were pleasant."

There was a remote quality about him that chilled her. A moment ago he was contentedly drinking coffee, yet now he appeared angry. Why? Gayle frowned. Surely Jake was not resenting her momentary inattention? Was he such an egotist?

"Yes"—Gayle's smile held a touch of mystery—"my thoughts were rather pleasant." *If* one could consider contemplation of a barroom brawl pleasant, she thought, silently qualifying her statement. As for Jake's being an egotist, it really had nothing at all to do with her—did it? Gayle leaned forward to place her empty cup—when had she drunk the contents?—and untouched cake on the table.

"Will you have more coffee?" she asked, avoiding his stare.

"I've *had* more coffee." Jake's grating tone brought her unwilling gaze back to his. "While you were off . . . reminiscing."

Moving suddenly, Jake shot to his feet to stride to the fireplace. Resting one forearm on the mantelpiece, he stared broodingly at the kindling, layed but unlit.

Gazing bleakly at his broad-shouldered back, Gayle cursed her own transparency. Had Jake read her thoughts? Gayle bit her lip. And, having read them, did he resent her speculation about his past? Obviously so, if his taut stance was any indication. Was an apology called for? Gayle sighed.

"I'm sorry, Jake."

"Are you?" Jake turned slowly, his eyes glinting with intent.

"Yes, of course!" Gayle wet suddenly parched lips, beginning to tremble as his intense gaze followed the gliding motion of her tongue. "If I've offended—"

"I'm interested in you," he said, cutting her apology off ruthlessly. "Very interested. And you're interested in me," he went on bluntly, ignoring the gasp that burst from her lips. "Don't pretend, Gayle. We're both too old for it." His mouth curved in a knowing smile. "There's a physical attraction between us—a very strong attraction. That in itself is hardly unusual; men and women are often sexually attracted to each other."

Gayle's trembling increased; she didn't like having her emotions probed . . . especially by a man! And most especially by this man. *Shut him up,* an inner voice warned.

"Jake, really, I . . ."

"I want more."

"What—" Gayle swallowed a bubble of panic. If he makes one move, takes one step, I'll scream for Marge, she thought wildly. Jake didn't move a muscle.

"I've known and explored the purely physical attraction." The very steadiness of his voice calmed her. "And now I want more from a woman." Jake's hesitation was brief, but long enough to add impact to his next sentence. "I think you're the woman I want more from."

At that instant Gayle would have begun screaming for all she was worth had she been able to get a sound past the constriction in her throat. Fortunately, Jake spared her the embarrassment of making an utter fool of herself by explaining just what he meant.

"I want to get to know you. I want you to know me. And not only in the Biblical sense." A wry smile curled his lips. "I've been Biblicalled seven ways from yesterday; I enjoyed it too." The smile vanished, leaving his face austere. "Now I need more." Removing his arm from the mantel, Jake straightened to his six foot plus, his gaze drilling into hers. "What I'm requesting, Gayle, is the right to pay court to you."

Gayle was still in a mild state of shock hours after Jake had bid her a very proper good night, reminding her that he would see her the following week for Thanksgiving dinner with Brant and Charley. Meanwhile, he'd added, shrugging into his topcoat, she was to carefully consider everything he'd said.

By three o'clock in the morning, wide awake and as jumpy as a drop of water skipping over a hot griddle, Gayle was beyond giving consideration to anything *but* what he'd said.

Jake Munger wants to pay court to me!

Gayle muffled a giggle born of hysteria. Giving up the battle with her tangled sheets, she abandoned the bed and slid her arms into the wide sleeves of a velour robe in a deep shade of burgundy. As she wrapped the robe tightly to her body, the tender skin on the underside of her arms brushed the velvety nap, causing a sensuous tingling all the way to her fingertips.

Never in her life had Gayle been so acutely aware of herself as a woman. Tentatively, nervously, she ran her palms down her sides from her waist to the top of her thighs.

Would Jake find her voluptuous form exciting? Or would he be repelled by the fullness of her figure?

What was she doing? Gayle's hands sprang away from her body as if scorched. Was she mad, thinking about whether or not she could please Jake Munger?

Discarding the robe, Gayle slipped under the rumpled covers and curled into a ball of misery.

Jake Munger is a predator, she instructed herself sternly, even if he's a soft-spoken one. Remember: the wild cat walks softly.

Oh God, Louis. I'm so scared.

Had he been wise or extremely stupid to reveal part of his hand to Gayle?

Hands jammed into his pockets, shoulders hunched, Jake stood at the window of his hotel suite staring at the sparse traffic moving along Broad Street. He'd taken his position at the wide window some three hours before; he'd asked himself the same question at least forty or fifty times.

Damn! Had he rushed his fences?

Sliding one hand from his pocket, he raised it to the back of his neck, under the loosened collar of his shirt. The suit jacket and tie had been flung onto a chair long since, and now he absently lifted his other hand to unfasten the buttons on his shirt.

Gayle.

An image rose to torment his mind. An image of lightly flushed cheeks, and gently curved lips, and satiny skin covering a gracefully arched neck. Jake's lips had tested the texture of that satiny neck. They ached to test the rest of her.

Jake's resolve hardened along with his body. Gayle d'Acier was the one. She was perfect for his plans;

more perfect than he'd ever dared to hope . . . for she suited him as well.

But . . . how did he go about jarring her out of the enraging habit of reminiscing about her husband? A feral smile pulled at Jake's lips, baring his hard, straight teeth.

Maybe he ought to begin by keeping her away from the house as much as possible.

Flower-patterned furniture indeed!

Chapter Five

Thanksgiving dawned picture-perfect—bright and clear and crisp as a new dollar bill. Rising early, Gayle shared croissants and coffee with Marge before they went their separate ways: Marge to the center-city apartment of her brother and sister-in-law; and Gayle to the sprawling ranch home Brant had had his father design for him when Charley became pregnant with their first child.

The ranch house was located west of the city, near Valley Forge, and as Gayle drove along the expressway that paralleled the Schuylkill River, she wondered if Jake would appear for dinner.

Strangely, confusingly, after the things he'd said to her the night they'd had dinner together, Jake had not contacted her in any way. And, after nearly a week of expecting either the phone or doorbell to ring at any moment, Gayle was filled with anxiety and frustration.

Her anxiety was due to the lack of communication between them; her frustration to the lack of an opportunity to tell him she wasn't interested in his suggestion that they get to know each other better.

Gayle had planned to tell Jake quite calmly that she did not care to be courted . . . regardless of the nights she lay awake, tormented by thoughts of him.

As she approached the ranch house, Gayle ran an appreciative glance over the clean lines of the redwood-and-glass structure, mentally applauding Louis's talent. The house suited Brant and Charley perfectly, and was large enough to accommodate the four children the couple hoped for.

After parking the car in front of the three-car garage, Gayle strolled along the walkway to the back entrance of the house, drawing deep breaths of the sharp, tangy fall air into her lungs.

"Happy Thanksgiving, Gayle." Charley met her at the sliding-glass doors that led into the dining room off the patio, her eyes bright with happiness and good health. "You're just in time to join me in a cup of coffee." Charley's welcoming smile grew into a grin. "Decaffeinated, of course."

"Happy Thanksgiving to you, too." Gayle returned Charley's greeting and her grin. "I'd love a cup of coffee—even if it is decaffeinated." Shrugging out of her fingertip-length, heather tweed coat, she shook her head as Charley reached for it. "I'll hang it up;

you pour the coffee. Where's Brant and the dynamo?" she asked, pausing in the archway to the hall.

"Having a shower together; they got back from their morning run only minutes ago."

Gayle stopped dead, her confusion comical. *"They were running?"* She laughed, visualizing Brant attempting to shorten his stride to match his two-year-old son's.

"Well, Brant was running." Charley laughed with Gayle. "He runs every morning with Stevie on his shoulders."

"You're kidding!" Gayle's eyes widened in amazement.

"Not at all. Brant's been running with Steve on his shoulders for over three months."

"Incredible." Picturing Brant jogging along with the sturdy two-year-old as a passenger on his shoulders, Gayle walked slowly to the hall closet. No wonder Brant's body was looking more muscular lately, she mused, hanging the coat inside the roomy closet.

"Hi, Mom!" The greeting came from behind her. "Happy Thanksgiving. Say hello to Gayle, Steve."

Turning to face Brant, Gayle managed to smile. Brant had first called her Mom seconds after the ceremony that had united her with his father. At the beginning, when she had hopes of conceiving Louis's child, the term hadn't bothered her. But now, with hope gone, the term took on different connotations; Gayle was terribly afraid that Brant would be the only one ever to call her Mom. Her smile hiding the twist of pain in her chest, Gayle returned his greeting while reaching for his son.

"Good morning, Brant." Lifting Steve out of his father's arms, Gayle hugged his sweet-smelling little body. "Oh, you're getting to be such a big boy," she crooned, closing her eyes as she nuzzled his silky hair. "Mommy told me you were running with Daddy." Blinking away the hot moisture gathering in her eyes, she raised her head to gaze lovingly into the boy's plump-cheeked, beautiful face. "Did you have fun?"

"Me runs fash." Steve's grin revealed tiny white teeth. "Fash as daddy," he added proudly.

"I'll bet you do!" Gayle exclaimed seriously. "And, if you continue growing like a little weed, you'll soon be as tall as Daddy!"

"And no wonder," Brant drawled, unable to conceal the pride in his voice. "The little squirt eats like a young horse."

"Eat, Daddy," Steve demanded hungrily.

"You see what I mean?" Brant grinned at Gayle. "I guess we'd better find this guy's mother to see if she has something to hold him over till lunch." Motioning Gayle to precede him, he led the way to the dining room.

"Steve hungy," the boy informed his mother as they stepped through the archway.

"Steve is always hun-gry," Charley articulated slowly, slanting a smile at Gayle as she deposited the child in his high chair. "Your coffee's there, Gayle." She nodded at the place next to the high chair at the large oval table. "Help yourself to the cinnamon rolls." Shifting her glance to her husband, she smiled warmly. "Darling, would you get Steve's toast from the kitchen while I pour his juice?"

The blatant adoration in Brant's expression as he looked at his wife and child before striding into the kitchen added another dimension to the pain inside Gayle. At that instant, she could see Louis in Brant.

This time Gayle hid her feeling by raising the cup to her lips and sipping at the strong brew. The last time she'd spent a holiday with Brant and Charley, the entire family had been there, including Louis; Charley's father, Stephen, for whom Steve had been named; and Charley's stepmother, Darleen, Stephen's former housekeeper. Remembrance brought a question to Gayle's mind.

"Aren't Stephen and Darleen coming for dinner?"

Pausing in the act of cutting toast into bite-size pieces for her son, Charley smiled ruefully and shook her head. "No. Dad's in London on a combined business and pleasure trip." Her expression softened as her laughter filled the spacious room. "Dad's on business," she qualified. "Darleen's having the pleasure of buying herself a new wardrobe!"

Was that the reason Jake had been invited to share what had always been a family day? Gayle mused, biting into a warm roll. More importantly, was Jake even going to show up?

The speculation caused conflict between Gayle's mind and body. Her mind cautioned against ever seeing him again; her body quickened at the prospect of his proximity. After nearly a week of the ongoing internal battle, Gayle was almost used to living with the conflict.

In the next moment, Brant inadvertently answered her question.

"Oh, I almost forgot. Jake called while I was in the bedroom, sweetheart." He smiled at Charley. "He said he'd try to get here for lunch, but, if he should be delayed, we're not to wait for him."

"This property must really be something," Charley opined contemplatively, "to keep Jake out there nearly a week."

Property? Out there? Gayle frowned into her cup. "Out where?" she asked, almost against her will.

"Is it out or is it up?" Charley inquired of her indulgently smiling mate.

"It's west," Brant supplied before giving his attention to Gayle. "Jake went to visit his parents last Saturday," he explained. "Apparently, his father had heard about a property he thought Jake might be interested in and made an appointment for Jake to look at it Monday morning." Brant smiled wryly. "I'd say his father's assumption proved correct, because Jake's still there. At least he was when he called me." He shrugged. "He might be on his way here now."

"I was really kinda hoping Jake would buy your place, Gayle." Charley's obvious disappointment seemed out of proportion to the circumstances. "I had hopes he'd remain in this area."

"Charlott." Brant's tone held warning. "You promised." His glance shot to Gayle, then back to Charley.

"I know," Charley sighed. "But . . ."

Every one of Gayle's internal sensors was sounding an alert. *She* was the subject of their obscure discussion, but in what way? Positive she would learn nothing from Brant, Gayle turned to Charley with her sternest expression.

"What did you promise not to do, Charley?" she asked with quiet determination.

Charley almost managed a look of innocence. "Why, nothing, nothing at all!"

Charley's guiltless tone clinched it for Gayle; her friend was up to something, and that something had everything to do with *her*.

"Char-ley." Gayle let her exasperation show in her tone. "Out with it."

"Oh!" Charley tossed her mane of gorgeous red hair. "I promised Brant I wouldn't play matchmaker."

"Matchmaker?" Gayle repeated softly. Then, as the meaning hit her, she squawked, "Matchmaker! With me and Jake Munger!"

"Well, why not?" Charley's shrug was eloquent.

"Why not? You of all women should know why not," she said grimly. "You were always the first to recognize a predator. And Jake Munger is a predator from the roots of his hair to the soles of his feet!"

"Whoa! Hold it!" Brant said, joining the battle. "Gayle, come on, now! Jake's a friend of mine. My best friend." He paused to shake his head as if he couldn't believe what he'd heard. "What have you got against him?"

Gayle opened her mouth to tell Brant, then closed it again. What could she say? She could hardly tell

Brant she *felt* threatened by Jake. And, from what Charley had just admitted, they would both probably be delighted if she told them Jake had asked for permission to court her. Permission indeed! In Gayle's opinion, having Jake ask permission was as ludicrous as having a lion ask permission to make a meal of her. But, could she explain that to Brant and Charley? Not likely. Gayle sighed; she really was on her own.

"I'm sorry," she finally responded when Brant frowned at her continued silence. "You're right. I have no reason to call him names."

Now Charley frowned too. "Gayle," she said slowly, "is there something Brant and I should know? Something you're not telling us?"

Gayle felt warmed by the protective note in Charley's tone and the concerned look on Brant's face. She also felt ashamed at upsetting them.

"No, nothing, really." She plastered a smile on her lips. "It's the raw . . ." She flexed her fingers, searching for the right word, then she gave up in defeat. "The raw look about him, I guess." She lifted her shoulders briefly. "Forget what I said, please. I'm just being silly."

Although the subject was dropped, Gayle was well aware it was not forgotten. It was a holiday, and her friends understandably wanted no sign of dissension in their home. But the interrogation would come at a later date, either by Brant or Charley, or both, and Gayle knew it. For the remainder of the morning, however, the conversation was kept strictly to light, general topics.

Jake didn't make it in time for lunch, which obviously disappointed Brant and Charley, but greatly relieved Gayle. It was early afternoon when he made his appearance; and his appearance set Gayle's pulses hammering.

Sweeping a glance over him during the hubbub of exchanged greetings, Gayle felt an aching emptiness begin to yawn inside. Jake's freshly shaved cheeks had the sheen of good health, his russet hair seemed to crackle with electricity, and his eyes glowed with inner satisfaction. His attire was elegantly casual: buff-colored slacks and a dark brown Harris tweed sport jacket over a pale-blue, finely knit pullover. He held a huge bouquet of gold- and bronze-colored chrysanthemums for Charley in one hand, a bottle of aged Scotch for Brant in the other, and a bunch of real turkey feathers for Steve in a leather-trimmed pouch.

Unreasonably, Gayle felt overlooked. Not that she expected or wanted Jake to bring her gifts, she assured herself. Still . . . Gayle would not allow herself to finish the thought.

Oddly, the nervousness Gayle had been living with for close to a week subsided with Jake's arrival. Confused by her own strange reaction to him, she looked on with longing as Jake hugged Charley in greeting. Then, her newfound calm was jolted as Jake raked her form with a gleaming gaze.

Suddenly Gayle felt that her soft wool skirt was too full for her well padded hips, and her long-sleeved blouse too frilly for her amply proportioned bosom. Unable to hold Jake's direct stare, Gayle hastily averted her gaze to give her attention to a very bouncy, excited Steve.

After the mild uproar caused by Jake's arrival, the rest of the day passed as holidays were supposed to but rarely did—idyllically.

In fact, there was only one instance that rattled Gayle's serenity, and that was when Jake dropped onto the floor to play with Steve late in the afternoon.

Observing their mutual enjoyment through lowered lashes, Gayle swallowed a sigh of longing as she watched the man romp with the giggling boy. She tried to tell herself that hunger was responsible for the sensation of emptiness she felt.

Conversation flowed easily as the afternoon became shrouded in darkness. They all joined a delighted Steve in the kitchen as he was fed his dinner. Then, to Gayle's amazement, Jake accompanied Brant to the nursery to help tuck the sleepy-eyed child into bed.

While the men occupied themselves with the bedtime ritual, Gayle helped Charley put the finishing touches to the traditional holiday meal, which the housekeeper had started earlier in the day.

"Gayle, what exactly is it about Jake that bothers you?" Charley probed gently as she stirred thickener into the aromatic turkey gravy.

Pausing in the act of slicing the log-shaped cranberry sauce, Gayle met Charley's eyes briefly before quickly glancing away.

"I . . . I really wish I hadn't mentioned it," Gayle responded softly, staring in consternation at the knife, which wobbled precariously in her trembling fingers. "I can't explain, exactly." Carefully placing the knife on the table, she sighed as she contemplated her trembling fingers. "Please, forget I mentioned it."

"But, Gayle! I—" Charley began, only to be interrupted by Jake's voice, which preceded him into the kitchen.

"Lord! Whatever it is you two are concocting in here, it smells delicious. I hope it will soon be ready for consumption."

"Thank you," Charley laughed. "And you guys are just in time to cart the food to the table."

When they were all seated around the dining-room table, Jake raised his glass to Charley. "I'd like to commend you on the excellent job you are doing with your son," he said seriously. "That kid is one happy cracker."

Begun on a note of laughter, the meal proceeded in shared conviviality from the shrimp cocktail appetizer to the spicy pumpkin pie dessert. Determined not to cause even a ripple of discord, Gayle stoically endured the assessing glances Jake sent gliding over her at regular intervals.

The tension that had simmered between them the night he'd taken her to dinner was back, tightening every one of Gayle's nerve endings and sending tingles down her spine. Never before had she looked forward to the end of a meal as she did that night, or sprung so eagerly to the task of clearing the table.

"After a meal like that, I need a brisk walk," Brant said only half-jokingly as he carried the meat platter into the kitchen. "Care to join me, Jake?"

Gayle held her breath until Jake murmured an offhand "sure," then let it out slowly as the men escaped kitchen duty by slipping out the back door.

"Have you said or done something to upset Gayle?"

Though every one of Jake's muscles tensed, his stride remained smooth and unbroken. "Why?" he asked calmly, not looking at Brant. "Has she complained about something I said or did?"

"No," Brant denied. "At least, not exactly."

"Well, what, exactly, did she say?"

"She referred to you as a predator," Brant informed him bluntly.

Jake not only looked at Brant this time, he stopped dead. "A what?" He expelled his breath with a snort of disbelief.

"You heard it, buddy." Brant shook his head while lifting his shoulders. "I couldn't fathom what she meant." His short burst of laughter held little humor. "And, like a woman, she refused to elaborate." Brant's lips twisted sardonically. "As I knew my adorable wife would very likely keep me up half the night with speculation, I decided to try prying some answers out of you." His smile hinted at apology. "Can you enlighten me?"

Unused to confiding in anyone, Jake was quiet for some minutes, then with a sigh of impatience he said starkly, "I ask for permission to pay court to your— uh—stepmother."

"Pay court?" Brant frowned at the antiquated term. "I don't understand."

"Apparently, neither did Gayle," Jake drawled. "A predator," he repeated softly. Then he said irritably, "Why a predator, I wonder?"

"Well, she also said there was a raw look about you, or some such." Brant shrugged. "There is obviously something about your appearance that bothers her. Hell, Jake, I don't know. Gayle's got this thing about men—always had."

"Thing?" Jake exclaimed softly. "What kind of thing?"

"She's afraid of men . . . I think."

Jake's eyes narrowed. "Yes," he murmured, "that would explain it." His tone hardened. "There must be a reason for her fear. What is it?"

"Damned if I know," Brant replied at once. "Perhaps Charley does, but I doubt it. Gayle's pretty closemouthed about her personal life."

Feeling as if he was on the edge of something important, Jake tingled with excitement. Nothing could have stopped him from probing at this point.

"Brant, you didn't pull the idea out of thin air," he said. "At some time or other, something she said gave you the impression that she feared men. I want to know what that something was."

"You know," Brant said dryly, "I'm beginning to think we should have taken time to put on our coats—it's damn cold out here."

"Friend, I don't care if you freeze your rump," Jake told him blandly. "We're not moving from this spot until you tell me what gave you the idea in the first place."

"You're a hard man," Brant chided.

"Right," Jake agreed promptly. "Now explain."

"It had to do with my father," Brant began, serenely unaware of the sudden tautening of Jake's body.

"*Your* father hurt Gayle in some way?" Jake asked in disbelief.

"You know better than that, Jake!" Brant sighed. "Will you let me explain in my own way . . . without interruptions?"

"My fingers are starting to get numb," Jake drawled, "but take your time."

"It was while I was—uh—still pursuing Charley." Brant smiled. "Gayle made an untimely visit to Charley's apartment one night while I was there and, instead of evicting me, as I fully expected she would, Charley asked me to stay, insisting *I* could be of more help to Gayle than she." Caught in his own memories, Brant's smile softened. Jake's sigh of impatience brought him back to the present. "Anyway, it seemed Gayle had a problem, and the problem was my father. The reason she had stopped by Charley's was to confer on ways to convince Dad that Gayle was perfect for him."

"And?" Jake urged.

"Naturally, I was skeptical. I asked Gayle bluntly if she was playing some sort of game or indulging in an older-man fantasy. Although Gayle denied any game-playing, surprisingly she did concede the possibility of a father-figure complex. It was after that admission that Gayle told me she couldn't relate to men in a one-to-one situation—that is, until she met my father."

"And her reason for being unable to relate?" Jake

again prompted impatiently, positive he was at last going to hear the reason for Gayle's wariness of him.

"She wouldn't say." Brant shrugged. "In fact, she denied the existence of any concrete reason. I didn't believe her then; I don't believe her now. But, what the hell, it is *her* business."

"And now I'm making it mine." Jake's adamant tone drew a sharp stare from Brant.

"You never did tell me what you meant by 'pay court' to her," he reminded Jake as the two of them turned to walk back to the warmth of the house.

"I intend to marry her."

Brant stopped in his tracks. "Does she know?" he asked with dry amusement.

"Apparently she hasn't figured it out yet. I suppose I'll have to draw her a diagram."

As they entered the house, both men were wearing secret smiles born of inner amusement.

Gayle turned from stacking the dishwasher as the back door opened. The sight of the odd smiles on Brant's and Jake's lips put her on guard immediately. There was such a conspiratorial look about them that Gayle was overwhelmed by an urge to run for the hills—or her car at the very least!

Am I getting paranoid? she asked herself.

As if attuned to her thoughts, Jake leveled his glittering gaze on her and lifted one brow teasingly.

Paranoid my foot! Gayle decided grimly. This man is on the hunt . . . and *I'm* the quarry!

Yet the shiver that crept along Gayle's spine owed more to excitement than fear. Spinning back to the dishwasher, she bit her lower lip in consternation. Was she totally mad? Surely she was not thrilled at the prospect of Jake in full pursuit of her?

Ignoring both men, Gayle finished loading the dishes and turned with a sigh of relief as Charley reentered the kitchen from the dining room.

"Wouldn't you know it?" Charley observed dryly. "The work's all done, and here they are . . . and very likely hungry again." Raising an elegantly arched brow at Brant, she quipped, "Were you hiding right outside the door all this time?"

"You insult me." Brant contrived to look offended. "There is not a devious bone in my body."

"Huh!" Charley snorted inelegantly. "I wouldn't be surprised to learn that the entire male form is constructed of devious bones. And you two have an especially devious look about you. What *have* you been up to?"

"My lips are sealed," Brant vowed, grinning at Jake.

Charley merely frowned; Gayle nearly panicked. The very fact that Jake didn't return Brant's grin seemed suspicious. Paranoid or not, Gayle felt positive that *she* had been the topic of discussion between Jake and Brant while they'd been having their after-dinner stroll.

What does the man want of me? she asked herself over and over again during the remainder of her visit. The obvious? Or . . . At this point, Gayle always backed away from any answers that might have presented themselves; in truth, she didn't *want* to know what Jake wanted of her.

At last, breathing a sigh of relief, Gayle made a move to leave. But her relief was short-lived.

"I have an early appointment tomorrow," Jake announced coolly. "So I'll be going too. I'll follow you home, Gayle. Make sure you get there safely."

Charley and Brant were vocal in their approval of Jake's idea. Gayle had to gulp back a bubble of hysteria, along with the question: Who will protect me from *him?*

Fifteen minutes later, Gayle found herself in her car, casting angry glances at the headlights reflected in her rearview mirror. As she steered the vehicle into her own driveway, she breathed a sigh, only to mutter a harsh expletive in the next second as the headlights reappeared in the mirror.

Braking in front of the garage doors, Gayle slammed out of the car, spun around and glared at those same lights as the long car glided to a stop beside her own.

"I thought you had an early appointment in the morning?" she snapped as Jake stepped out of the vehicle.

"I do," he responded calmly, circling the front end to get to her.

"Then why . . ." she began in exasperation.

"I wanted to talk to you." Jake's smooth voice overrode her query.

"We have nothing to talk about." Gayle prayed the finality in her tone would discourage him; at the same time she knew her prayer would be ignored. She was correct.

"I think we do," Jake insisted softly. "Shall we go inside?"

"I think not," Gayle said, denying both his assumption and his question.

"I intend to have this discussion, Gayle." Now Jake's tone held finality. "Even if it's over the sound of your chattering teeth. So, make up your mind. Do we talk out here, where you'll become chilled? Or inside, where you can get comfortable?"

"Ooh!" Gayle bit back the curse that rose to her lips. Raising her hands in a gesture of defeat, she stormed away from him toward the house, gritting her teeth at the mocking sound of his soft laughter.

Inside the house, Gayle flung her coat at the parson's bench by the wall and strode into the living room without pausing.

"Okay, get it over with." Turning to face him, she lifted her chin defiantly. "But make it quick," she warned.

"Feisty all of a sudden, aren't you?" Jake taunted, strolling to within inches of her. "Or is your show of temper an act?" he wondered aloud. "Why are you afraid of me, Gayle?"

"I'm not!" Gayle denied hotly—much too hotly. She forced herself to meet his eyes, then immediately regretted it. Needing to put distance between them, she slowly backed away from him.

Jake slowly stalked her retreating form. When her spine made contact with the mantelpiece, Gayle cried in desperation, "What do you want of me, Jake?"

"An answer to the request I made of you last

week," Jake replied softly, again walking to within inches of her. He smiled playfully, revealing even white teeth. "I want to come a-courting."

"But . . . but, why?" Gayle could not deny the thread of fear in her tone. "We've only just met! I know nothing about you!"

"What would you like to know?" He was so close, his warm breath caressed her lips. "All you have to do is ask—anything, anything at all."

For a long second, Gayle's mind went completely blank. Then, amazingly, she was tempted to ask for the feel of his mouth on hers. Shocked by the sudden, overriding need, Gayle grasped at the first thought that came into her mind.

"I don't even know what you do for a living!" she blurted artlessly.

A burst of laughter exploded from Jake's throat. "Oh, Gayle, you are absolutely precious!" he exclaimed when his laughter had subsided to a chuckle. "I design computers for a living," he supplied.

The Mung!

For five full seconds Gayle stared at Jake in disbelief; then she slowly closed her eyes. Holy night! There was a Mung computer residing in pride of place on the receptionist's desk at her law firm! The small computer was one of the few that was appropriate for both personal and professional use, and its designer had been hailed as a genius. From what Gayle had heard, Jake had realized millions on the Mung! And he had produced several innovative machines since the original—all of them bearing the Mung name.

"Are you going to say something, or simply stare at

me as though I'd just dropped in from another planet?" Jake's teasing tone jolted Gayle out of her reverie.

"The Mung?" Gayle whispered in a tone of near awe.

"'Fraid so," Jake drawled. "But don't let the information throw you. I am a man, Gayle."

I'll say, she concurred mutely, and then some! But Jake's reference to himself as a man stirred memories, memories of articles linking him with several well known women in high places. Still gazing into his compelling eyes, Gayle followed her train of thought to its natural conclusion: What could a man like Jake want with *her?*

Positive she knew the answer, and suddenly furious because of it, Gayle went on the attack.

"For what reason would a man like *you* even consider paying court to a woman like me?" Glaring at him, Gayle felt a curious leap in her pulse rate when Jake smiled.

"Marriage, of course."

Chapter Six

Of course. What else? Marriage. Oh, God!

The thoughts ricocheted inside Gayle's head like a wildly fired bullet.

"You're crazy . . . no, *I'm* crazy! You are asking me to marry you?" Gayle was babbling, she *knew* she was babbling. Still, she couldn't halt the rush of words. "No, no way." She shook her head fiercely. "You're playing some kind of game here . . . aren't you?" Not waiting for a response, she chattered on. "I don't like or appreciate these kinds of games, Jake. It is cruel and un—"

"Gayle! Will you shut up." Jake didn't raise his voice; but then, Jake didn't have to raise his voice. Though quietly spoken, every word held authority. Gayle was silent. "What the hell is it about me that terrifies you?" he asked with genuine concern. Lifting his hand, he touched the very tip of his index finger to her cheek, setting her skin on fire as he drew a line to the corner of her mouth. "I'm sorry if I've upset you. I hadn't planned on proposing until *after* the courting."

"Planned?" Gayle snatched at the one word. "Wh—what do you mean, planned?"

Jake sighed. "I knew when I left you last week that I was going to ask you to marry me . . . eventually. I never dreamed it would be *this* soon, or in this way."

"But why?" Gayle cried, curling her nails into her palms to counteract the shivers his touch ignited. "Why would you want to marry me?"

"Because you are exactly what I'm looking for in a wife," he answered bluntly. "You have every quality I require."

"Every quality?" Gayle repeated blankly. Whatever happened to mutual trust, and respect, and . . . and love? she wondered bleakly. "I don't understand. What qualities do you require?"

"Well, you are a lovely woman." He smiled. "But, you knew that, didn't you?"

Gayle shook her head vigorously; she had never considered herself more than passingly attractive. Still, she had no objection to hearing him compliment her.

"You are," Jake insisted. "Very lovely. But beauty itself was never one of my major considerations." This time Jake's smile held just a hint of arrogance. "I have known many beautiful women." The smile turned sardonic. "I even married one of them." His hesitation was barely noticeable, but Gayle noticed.

"That's beside the point. I had determined that this time I'd look below the surface for more enduring qualities like gentleness, and serenity, and, most importantly, a true affection for children. It quickly became evident to me that *you* possessed every one of those qualities."

On the horizon of Gayle's consciousness the dawn was beginning to break. Jake Munger was looking for a mother for his children! And *she* was his choice for the role!

Appalled, Gayle stared at Jake in sheer disbelief. Did the man truly not realize how very insulting he was being? She had had a normal, *loving* relationship with one husband. Could he honestly believe she'd actually consider, even for one moment, any other kind of marriage?

Denying the existence of the twist of pain in her chest, Gayle stared at Jake out of eyes devoid of all expression.

"I'd like you to leave now, please." Gayle barely recognized her own voice, so icy had it become.

"Gayle, you're taking this the wrong way," Jake said with quiet urgency.

"Really?" There was a tiny catch in her voice. "How could you possibly delude yourself into thinking I'd take an insulting proposal like this any other way?"

"Insulting!" Jake straightened abruptly. "There is not one damn thing insulting about my proposal!" His eyes flashed. Fully expecting a show of violence, Gayle steeled herself for the blast. It didn't come.

With visible effort, Jake forced himself to relax. Gayle caught herself exhaling slowly in unison with him.

"I was offering you total honesty, Gayle," Jake finally said quietly. "Honesty can hardly be called an insult."

"You were offering me the position of governess to your children!" Gayle corrected heatedly.

"I asked you to be my wife." Jake enunciated each word through stiffened lips. "I am offering you my name."

Jake's tone chilled Gayle's body to the bone and left her with little doubt about the honor he thought he'd bestowed upon her. His name. On reflection, Gayle had to admit that the name Munger was indeed an honorable one—at least in the business world. Did she owe Jake an apology? Gayle wasn't quite sure.

"And I am offering you my children."

After his long pause, Jake's quiet statement had the effect of a shout. Offering her his children! Gayle opened her mouth, then closed it again. Her heart twisted with longing. Children . . . Jake's children! The connotations were both exciting and frightening. Gayle did not know this woman inside who suddenly yearned to say yes.

"Are you going to respond at all?" Jake's tightly controlled voice snapped her to attention. "What's it going to be? Yes? No? Maybe? Go to hell?"

"Jake, I . . . we . . . Oh, how can you expect me to answer?" Gayle demanded. "We know so little about each other. I can't possibly make an intelligent decision without . . ." Gayle's voice trailed away as she realized what she was saying. Was she actually considering his preposterous proposal?

"I'm not asking for a decision now, Gayle." His taut body visibly relaxing, Jake smiled. "If you'll remember, the original request was for permission to court you." Jake's smile widened. "I didn't use the expression 'court' on a whim, as I feel sure you suspected I did." His smile vanished and his tone went soft. "No, Gayle, what I was requesting was time to learn about each other, time that used to be called courting. *Now* can you give me an answer?"

There were complexities to this man Gayle had never expected. Intrigued, Gayle allowed temptation to overrule common sense. With a sigh that signaled her capitulation, she gave him a tremulous smile.

"All right, Jake. You have my permission to . . . call."

"When?"

Jake's fingertip was on the move again, gliding across her cheek, circling the edge of her ear, making mincemeat of what little composure Gayle had left.

"Tomorrow?"

Jake had moved even closer to her. Gayle could feel his warm breath feather her lips, heating them, luring them to touch his own.

"Gayle?"

His mouth was poised over hers, waiting, waiting. Consumed by an urgency she had never experienced before, Gayle whimpered softly. She *had* to have his mouth.

"Yes, tomorrow."

Jake's hard male lips brushed hers lightly, so very

lightly, then settled as if they had found a long-sought home. His kiss was exquisite in its gentleness, frustrating in its briefness. Gayle could not prevent a moan of protest when he raised his head.

"Tomorrow," Jake whispered against her cheek, cupping her face with his hands, "may I call you at the office?"

"Yes." At that instant, Gayle would have agreed to just about any suggestion he cared to make. Her body, her entire being, felt more alive than at any other time in her life. Silently she willed him to crush her to him. Disappointment cut deep as Jake dropped his hands and stepped back.

"I must go." Though several inches now separated them, Gayle imagined she could feel the touch of his gaze on her mouth. "I really do have an early appointment." Turning, he strode to the middle of the room, then spun back around. "You won't change your mind?"

"No, Jake, I won't change my mind," Gayle assured him softly.

The sigh that Jake expelled could only be discerned in the movement of his chest. A self-mocking smile flashed across his lips.

"I'll call you at lunchtime. Okay?"

"Okay."

Jake stood perfectly still for one very long, heart-stopping moment; then he whipped around and strode from the room.

Moving carefully, Gayle sank into the nearest chair and sat staring at the archway Jake had just walked through. How strange, she mused, blinking herself back to reality. How absolutely bizarre! After all her fears concerning him, Jake had been satisfied with one chaste kiss! And *she* had had to fight the urge to twine her fingers in his hair and clamp his mouth to hers!

Shaking her head in wonderment, Gayle drifted more than walked up the short flight of stairs to her bedroom. Dazed and confused by sensations so alien to her nature, she let her clothes lie where they dropped and slid into bed nude—another first. Her lips aching, her body hungering for some elusive something she couldn't even put a name to, she curled into a ball and, amazingly, slipped into sleep within minutes.

Jake was deceptively relaxed-looking as he stretched his length out on the one comfortable chair in the sitting room of his hotel suite. He rested his head against the chair back and closed his eyes.

Gayle had responded to him—he knew that. He had felt her response in the tremor in her cheek when he'd touched her with his finger, and in the softening of her lips when he'd kissed her. But there was a fear in her. Jake knew that as well. And even though Brant had told him Gayle was afraid of most men, Jake also knew that at the present all her fear was centered in him.

Play it delicately, Jake advised himself, or you are going to lose her.

A few months ago, two weeks ago, the sure knowledge of losing a woman wouldn't have bothered Jake at all; he would have shrugged his shoulders and gone on to more important things—like his work, and the company that had evolved from it.

Now, to find himself not only bothered, but unable to sleep as well, was damned annoying. Nevertheless, Jake was both bothered and unable to sleep . . . and not for the first time, either.

The problem that kept Jake wakeful was strategy. He would have preferred to lay his cards on the table, bargaining if necessary to achieve his goal. That was the approach he would have taken a week ago.

But one day less than that week Jake had had dinner with Gayle, experiencing an attraction so powerful it had left him wary and uncertain. Not that Jake was at all uncertain about what he wanted, he knew exactly what he wanted. By the end of the evening he'd met her, he knew he wanted Gayle for the mother of his two young daughters. By the end of the evening he'd taken her to dinner, he knew he wanted Gayle for himself.

His uncertainty was in how to achieve his goals. Every molecule in Jake's body urged him to swoop and conquer, while every brain cell he possessed cautioned against precipitous action.

Jake hadn't really needed Brant's remarks about Gayle's attitude to men; he had made the same deduction after being in her company less than an hour. The only error in analysis he'd made was in attributing her distant attitude to grief over the loss of her husband, rather than a deeply rooted fear of men in general.

Deciding to play it cool, Jake determined to be the model of propriety while courting Gayle.

Easing his body out of the chair, Jake strolled into
the bedroom. After absently unbuttoning his shirt, he
shrugged it off his shoulders, then rubbed one palm
over the diamond-shaped mat of hair on his chest.

Damn! he groaned as passion stirred deep inside. I
hope to God massive doses of circumspect behavior
cure this phobia of hers quickly!

Gayle decided that Murphy's law was in full effect
Friday morning: everything that could go wrong did.
By eleven-thirty she was alternately snapping at her
secretary and glaring at the phone. She was unsure,
even in her own mind, whether she wanted it to ring
or not. The last thing she needed was to have David
saunter into her office with an invitation to lunch. So,
naturally, that was exactly what she got.

"I've made a reservation at the café in the hotel
Hershey," he said, unabashedly flashing his boyish
grin. "I don't know about you, but for me a working
day following a holiday is always a shambles." David
managed a sigh of despair. "Nothing, but *nothing,* is
going right for me today."

Delighted to discover a fellow sufferer, Gayle
smiled in commiseration. "And here all this time I
was thinking *I* was the only one having trouble getting
my act together today." She smiled back at him as she
gazed into his eager face. "I'm sorry, David, but I
have a previous engagement for lunch."

"With whom?" he demanded. Then, smiling sheep-
ishly, he immediately tacked on, "Gayle, I'm sorry."
Raking his hand through his stylishly trimmed hair, he
wet his lips nervously. "I know I have no right to

question your movements, but . . . dammit, Gayle! You know how I feel about you!"

"David, I like you, you know that, but . . ." Gayle broke off with a deep sigh.

"But there is no spark between us. Right?"

"I'm sorry." Gayle caught her bottom lip with her teeth. What else could she say to him? Gazing up at him through eyes soft with concern, she sighed again. There was nothing more *to* say. There was no spark of anything but friendship between them. There never had been.

Standing in front of her desk, not moving at all, David stared at Gayle sadly. The sudden, shrill summons of the phone set him into motion.

"I'll get out of here now, but"—his smile brightened—"I hope you realize I intend to keep trying?"

Reaching for the phone, Gayle shook her head at him. "Oh, David . . ." The persistent ringing checked her words. As she moved to pick up the receiver, David wheeled around and walked out of the office, closing the door with a soft click.

"How did I manage to get you without going through your secretary?" Jake drawled teasingly when Gayle gave her name.

"Janine is out to lunch," Gayle replied, trying to ignore the fluttery beat of her heart. What had David said about sparks? "And don't you dare make the obvious remark, either."

Jake's soft laughter did strange and wonderful things to her. "I never go for the obvious, Gayle."

Oddly, Gayle had the distinct impression that Jake

was implying a lot more than he had actually said. While she was considering the possibility of a hidden meaning, Jake laughed again.

"I'll explain it to you someday," he promised in a low tone. "Are you free to join me for lunch?"

Gayle blinked at his abrupt briskness. "Yes."

"Good." There was a new quality to his tone, a purring satisfaction. "I've been in conference all morning at the Hershey. In fact, I'm in the café at this moment. Why don't you jump into a cab and come over."

The café at the Hershey! The coincidence was too much. Gayle laughed softly. "All right, Jake. I'll leave at once. You may order a drink for me."

"Certainly," Jake said at once, then asked, "Did I say something amusing?"

"I'll explain it to you someday," Gayle drawled huskily, using his own words. Suddenly feeling light-hearted, she added, "I'm in the mood for a glass of champagne with my lunch. Okay?"

"Champagne?" Jake murmured. "Honey, as long as you ask in that sexy voice, you can have anything your little heart desires." His pause was infinitesimal. "Beginning and ending with me."

So carefully did he replace the receiver, Gayle wasn't aware that he'd done so till she heard the dial tone. A tiny curl of excitement unwound deep inside as she grabbed her purse from her bottom desk drawer and went hurrying from her office.

Gayle saw him the minute she walked through the hotel doors. Jake was sitting at one of the tables placed at the rail of the balcony that jutted out over the hotel lobby. His steady gaze was on the people coming and going through the hotel entrance.

Impulsively, she lifted her hand in a jaunty wave, smiling as she mouthed "hello." Jake seemed to freeze for an instant; then he smiled back as he pushed out his chair and stood up.

Gayle came to an abrupt stop below his table, her breath growing shallow as she stared up at him. Jake returned her stare, his eyes mysterious with promises of . . . what?

How long she stood transfixed, unmindful of the people jostling her as they hurried by, Gayle hadn't the vaguest idea. Captured by the depths of his eyes, she might have waited indefinitely had he not released her by calling softly.

"Come up here."

Gayle obeyed without thought. The elevator swept her up to the second floor. When she stepped out of the car, he was waiting for her, a half-smile on his chiseled lips.

"You look stunning without lipstick and your hair all windblown like that," he said quietly, taking her hand to lead her to their table.

Gayle's other hand flew first to her mouth, then to her hair. She'd been in such a rush to join him, she hadn't even thought about checking her makeup! And a gust of the fall breeze had caught her as she stepped out of the cab.

"Is there a ladies room?" she asked. Idiot, she berated herself, there's *always* a ladies room, for heaven's sake!

"I *told* you, you look stunning." Jake laughed,

refusing to release her hand. "I *meant* it." Sliding the chair next to his away from the table with his free hand, he said, "Sit down, Gayle. The waiter will be here to take our order in a moment."

There was a large menu lying at her place, and as Gayle lifted it a waiter approached the table carrying a wine bucket. Sticking out from the top was the neck of a very expensive bottle of French champagne. Smothering a gasp of shock, Gayle watched, bemused, as the waiter went through the uncorking ritual.

"For lunch?" she queried softly after the waiter had filled their glasses and departed, promising to return for their order momentarily.

"Why not?" Jake's shrug was casually elegant. "I wanted to celebrate."

"Celebrate!" Gayle laughed. "Celebrate what?"

"The first date in our courtship," Jake replied simply, raising his glass in silent salute to her. His gaze held hers while he sipped the wine. "I'm hoping it will be the first in a very short courtship."

Ready to sip from her own glass, Gayle gulped instead, feeling the bubbles tingle all the way down her throat. Jake was dead serious, and she knew it. For an instant panic gripped her; then she forced herself to relax. Jake had not pressed his advantage the night before, and he had definitely had one, she remembered too well.

Sipping thirstily, Gayle studied him over the rim of her glass. Jake had not changed since the evening she'd met him; he still looked rough-hewn and dangerous. Yet, aside from that one slip when he'd caressed the pulse in her throat with his lips and whispered urgently, "Come to bed with me," he had made no demands. Could she trust him? Gayle asked herself warily.

"Don't close up on me, Gayle," Jake said in a raw voice, making her wonder if he had guessed her thoughts. "I said I was *hoping* the courtship would be short," he went on tightly. "I didn't say anything about forcing the issue."

"Jake, I'm not sure if this is wise." Gayle wet her lips. "It's been such a short time since Louis—"

"It's been nearly a year," Jake interrupted harshly.

Gayle's entire body stiffened. At her withdrawal, Jake reached across the table and swallowed her hand in his.

"You are a young woman, Gayle." Jake's grip tightened as she tried to draw her hand away. "You can't grieve forever," he insisted softly, more gently. "Keep your memories, but let him go."

"I . . . I loved him so." Because her eyes were moist with tears, Gayle could not quite identify the spasm of emotion that moved over Jake's face, but she could feel the grip of his fingers around hers.

"I know you did," he finally murmured. "And you will probably always love him, or at least the memory of him. But that doesn't mean you have to stop living."

"I haven't stopped living!" Gayle protested.

Jake's eyes narrowed in contemplation. "No, perhaps you haven't stopped . . . simply because you really never started." He smiled when she gasped. "Really living takes more than going through the motions, Gayle."

Jake was hitting too close to home. "I assure you, I did not go through the motions during my marriage, Mr. Munger." She tried to get up. Jake anchored her by tightening his hold on her hand.

"Stay where you are." Jake's voice had taken on a tone Gayle had not heard from him before, a tone of a man used to giving commands and having them obeyed. "All right, if I was out of line, I'm sorry."

"*If* you were out of line?" Gayle again tugged against his hold unsuccessfully. "Will you let go of me, please?" she demanded through gritted teeth.

"No." Jake no longer sounded perturbed. In fact, he had the temerity to sound amused. "We haven't had lunch yet."

Furious, yet strangely exhilarated, Gayle glared at him. Jake smiled beguilingly. Gayle sighed in defeat. When Jake smiled in that manner, all the fight went out of her.

"You're a terrible man!" she muttered.

"But not too terrible," Jake retorted humorously. "I *did* spring for the champagne."

Wanting to laugh, but determined not to, Gayle swept the room with a glance. "Where *is* that waiter?" she complained. "I'm starving!"

The moment she said it, she knew it was true. She was suddenly very hungry. For lunch? Or for life?

"Anything appeal to you?" Jake asked blandly. "The assorted seafood salad? A mushroom omelet? Me?"

His tone was so devilish, Gayle couldn't help but respond to his teasing. "You?" Her eyebrows arched high in exaggeration. "Even charbroiled, I think you'd be as tough as old army boots!"

Leaning close to her, Jake whispered, "Would you like a test bite?"

"I think I'll settle for the seafood salad," Gayle said, declining his offer sweetly.

"You don't know what you're missing," Jake teased. "I don't give many the opportunity to sink their teeth in me."

Gayle shuddered delicately. What would his skin taste like? she mused, amazed at the longing that circled her chest like a constricting band.

"I'll pass, thank you," she finally choked out.

"Well, consider it, if you like," he murmured so the waiter coming toward their table couldn't overhear. "I'll extend the invitation again tonight . . . late tonight."

Chapter Seven

Tonight? Late tonight?

Distractedly fingering the napkin draped over her lap, Gayle ordered the seafood salad. Tonight? What *was* Jake planning for tonight? Inside her, anticipation vied with caution. Anticipation won, making her blood run with an unfamiliar eagerness. Positive Jake would reveal his plans for the evening when he was good and ready, and not one second before, Gayle refrained from asking about them by raising her glass to her lips.

As the waiter walked away from the table, Jake's glance collided with hers. The intensity of his gaze brought all the excitement and tension flooding back in full, sizzling force. Emptying her glass with a few deep swallows, Gayle held it out for him to refill. As he poured the golden liquid, a teasing smile twitched at the corners of his mouth.

"This is potent stuff, honey," Jake advised softly. "Don't you think you'd better go easy? At least until you've put some food inside yourself?"

"Yes, I suppose so," Gayle murmured vaguely, intrigued by his casual endearment. Jake's chuckle alerted her to the dreamy sound of her voice. "Yes," she repeated firmly, placing the fragile glass on the table. "I feel a little fuzzy-minded already." That her fuzziness was due to his proximity and not the wine, Gayle prudently kept to herself.

The salad was delicious; at least Gayle felt sure it would have been delicious if she had tasted it! It was with a jolt of surprise that she noted that not only the salad but the garnishes of melon slices and fruit had disappeared from the plate!

"Now we'll kill the bottle," Jake declared softly, filling both glasses to the rim. "And I'll fill you in on my plans for this evening," he added, his eyes gleaming with amusement.

Lifting the glass carefully to avoid spilling a drop, Gayle sipped daintily. "Why do I have this nasty suspicion you're up to mischief?"

"Who? Me?" Jake laughed. "It's been a very long time since I've been accused of being up to that." He grinned. "A lot of other things, maybe, but not mischief." His grin gave her a good idea of exactly what those other things might have been.

Her cheeks growing hot, Gayle lowered her lashes demurely, innocently unaware of the enticement of her action. When she raised her eyes again, it was to discover that Jake's attention was riveted on her.

"You *are* beautiful," he whispered for her ears alone. "And unbelievably natural."

Flustered, flattered, and frantic all at the same time, Gayle felt her face flame even more. "Jake, please! Someone might hear you!"

"They don't have to hear me, not if they have eyes in their heads." Without moving, his glance swept the tables around them. "And they most certainly do," he added grimly.

Restraining the urge to follow his sweeping glance, Gayle frowned. "What are you talking about?"

"Tell me you haven't noticed the admiring stares from the men in the vicinity?" he drawled in a disbelieving tone. "Some instinct warns me those men were not admiring *me*," he added drolly.

This time it was impossible to prevent her gaze from circling the area. Shockingly, delightfully, her glance was met by more than one pair of male eyes—one man even had the audacity to wink at her! Stunned, Gayle returned her gaze to the very masculine male seated opposite her. Now Jake was scowling. Gayle absolutely loved it! Could Jake possibly be jealous? The mere idea was mind-boggling!

Before she could get too carried away, Gayle chided, "You still haven't told me your plans for this evening."

Deliberately moving his head this time, Jake met the stares of the surrounding males with a glittering, narrow-eyed glare; every pair of eyes was hastily averted. Satisfied, he shifted that glittering stare back to Gayle.

"How about skipping over the state line into Maryland for a quicky marriage ceremony?"

"You're not serious!" Gayle's wide eyes were met by a drilling stare.

"No?" he refuted. "Try me."

Gayle gulped more of her wine in an attempt to quench her sudden thirst. Incredibly, she was suddenly on fire with the need to take him at his word and indeed *try him*. The image that suddenly commandeered her mind was so explicit, Gayle felt herself blush all over. What was *wrong* with her? she wondered dazedly, draining her glass. Sensuality was abhorrent to her—wasn't it?

"Well?"

Jake's question shattered Gayle's bemusement. Blinking away the sensual mist clouding her mind, she focused her gaze on his attentive expression.

"You need to ask?" she hedged.

"I thought not a moment ago," he replied consideringly. "But now? Yes, I need—no, must—ask." Abruptly leaning forward, he said hoarsely, "Come, run away and marry me, Gayle."

Gayle swallowed against a tightness in her throat. "Jake, please." Gayle's voice sounded every bit as hoarse as his had. "You told me"—she wet her lips, aware that his eyes followed the movement of her tongue—" you assured me you wanted time to get to know me. I . . ."

"I know." Jake's smile held self-mockery. "I got

carried away for a minute there." He shrugged. "Okay, back to the original plans for tonight." His eyes were glowing again with inner amusement. "How would you like to go Christmas shopping with me?"

Christmas shopping? For an instant, Gayle's mind went completely blank, then she repeated the thought aloud. "Christmas shopping? This evening?"

"The day after Thanksgiving *is* the traditional kick-off day for Christmas shopping . . . isn't it?" Jake asked softly.

"Well, yes, but . . ."

"And this *is* the day after Thanksgiving . . . isn't it?" He was now actually purring. The velvet sound of his voice found its way inside Gayle's defenses.

"Yes, but . . ." Gayle paused warily. "Why do *you* want to go?"

Jake laughed, from low in his throat. Gayle was done for—and she knew it. "I have shopping to do," he said with great simplicity. "I'd appreciate your opinion on my selections."

Was there a woman alive who could resist a man who admitted to needing her help? Gayle asked herself. If there was, she certainly wasn't the one, she immediately answered. The question resolved, Gayle smiled brightly.

"I'd absolutely adore helping you spend your money," she teased. Then she added more seriously, "As long as it's not on a gift for another woman."

Unaware of exactly how much she'd revealed to him with her qualifying statement, Gayle frowned at Jake's bark of delighted laughter, then thrilled at his reassuringly prompt reply.

"There is no other woman, Gayle." Jake's glance drifted slowly over her from waist to hair. "Except, of course, for my mother and sisters-in-law. I *really* require assistance in the selection of gifts for them. So, then, what do you say? Are you game?"

Gayle laughed. "You *do* realize it will be a fight through the crowds every inch of the way, don't you?"

"Yes." Jake nodded, then frowned. "Well, actually, no. I've never gone shopping on the day after Thanksgiving." His frown gave way to a grin. "It'll be a learning experience."

"It will be that!" Gayle grinned back. "What time would you like me to be ready?"

"I've been thinking about that," Jake said slowly. "Do you have something pressing in the office this afternoon?"

"No." Gayle shook her head. "I was planning to catch up with the paperwork, so I told Janine not to schedule any appointments for today. Why?"

"Don't go back at all," Jake urged, like a boy suggesting that she play hooky from school. "We'll get an early start on the shopping, then have a quiet dinner." His slow smile did devastating things to her pulse rate. "If you're good, I'll take you dancing after dinner." The smile grew wicked. "And if you're very good, I'll kiss you good night when I take you home."

"Indeed!" Gayle murmured primly. "And is the promise of a kiss supposed to excite me?"

"Indeed not!" Jake mocked her tone. "But I think the actual kiss might."

Gayle contained herself for a full five seconds, then

burst out laughing. "Jacob Munger, you are a bad man!" she gasped, trying to catch her breath.

"Well," Jake drawled. "You know what they say a woman needs on a cold winter's night—don't you?"

"What?" Gayle asked warily, positive she was walking into a punch line; Jake didn't disappoint her.

"A good book or"—his voice went low—"a very bad man."

"That does it!" Fighting a fit of the giggles, Gayle slid back her chair. "And for your information, sir," she went on as he escorted her from the restaurant, "winter hasn't started yet."

"But it will, and soon," he murmured close to her ear as he helped her with her coat. "And I'm really looking forward to those long, cold nights."

"Now stop that!" Hiding a smile, Gayle strode through the entrance doors, then paused, glancing at him inquiringly. "Where do you want to start?"

"What a leading question!" Jake groaned. As Gayle narrowed her eyes at him warningly, he held up a hand in self-protection. "All right, I'll behave myself. And I'll even allow you the choice of shops. Where would *you* like to start?"

"Wanamaker's," Gayle replied promptly.

"Wherever." Jake shrugged. "Any particular reason for Wanamaker's?"

"Of course, silly," she chided. "I want to see the light show."

Silly.

A smile teasing his strongly defined lips, Jake

sipped at the sour mash in the stubby glass he held lightly in his big hand. How long had it been since anyone had had the temerity to call *him* silly?

The smile expanded to reveal hard, white teeth. As far as memory served—and memory served Jake very well—no one had ever addressed him so.

Laughing softly, deep in his throat, Jake sauntered to the wide window in the sitting room of his hotel suite. Come to that, he mused, how long had it been since he'd actually derived enjoyment out of shopping . . . for anything? He had always detested searching the stores in quest of the perfect gift, or even the required articles of clothing for himself.

Yet, that very same afternoon he had not merely tolerated the chore, he had found it extremely pleasurable! And all because of the company of a woman who dared call him silly.

Jake sipped at the drink again, savoring the fire that trickled down his throat. One woman. The smile on Jake's lips took a gentle curve as he conjured an image of Gayle d'Acier, her face flushed from laughter, her eyes sparkling with delight as he'd groaned under the weight of the steadily increasing load of packages she fiendishly dropped into his arms.

His mood as mellow as the whiskey, Jake reflected on the hours they'd spent together.

Hands clasped in companionship, they'd strolled the few blocks that separated the hotel from the large department store. True to Gayle's warning, the crush of people inside the store forced their leisurely stroll to a crawl. Laughing at his exaggeratedly appalled expression, Gayle had inquired sweetly where he wished to begin.

"The toy department," Jake replied, surveying the area with genuine interest.

"The toy department!" Gayle exclaimed, her dark eyes gleaming with amusement. "You *are* a glutton for punishment!"

"How so?" he demanded, controlling the urge to join her laughter.

The look Gayle bestowed on him was pitying. "You are aware of the fact that Santa Claus made his yearly appearance during the Thanksgiving Day parade yesterday, are you not?" she asked.

"Sure," Jake responded, shrugging. "So?"

"So, the toy department will be a bedlam—kids of all ages, itching and squirming to whisper into Santa's ear. Are you positive you're up to facing a horde of pushing, chattering, wailing youngsters?"

"If Guntar Williams can face the lions," Jake drawled, "I can face a horde of kids." With a casual wave of his hand, he indicated the crowded bank of elevators. "Carry on, intrepid shopper; I'll follow wherever you care to lead."

And follow he had, pushing and shoving, murmuring "I beg your pardon's" and "excuse me's" along with the most experienced bargain-hunters. Though he grumbled at regularly timed intervals, in truth Jake loved every minute of it. And, if the light shining from her eyes was any evidence, so did Gayle.

The afternoon was on the wane and the mound of packages he was carrying had grown into a veritable mountain when Jake literally cried "cease and desist."

"You're tired?" Gayle asked in a honey-coated tone, fluttering her lashes very effectively.

"I'm parched!" Jake retorted with a grin. "Let's dump this junk somewhere and find the nearest bar."

"Junk!" Gayle choked. "By my estimate, you have spent in the neighborhood of two thousand dollars! How dare you call it junk?"

"I'm extremely courageous?" Jake batted his blunt lashes with less effectiveness and was amazed at his uncharacteristic behavior. Always before, if he bothered to flirt with a woman at all, it was in a subtly sexual way. This . . . this fun flirting, for want of a more descriptive expression, was proving to be exactly that—pure fun. Sadly, Jake couldn't even remember the last time he'd indulged in the business of having fun.

"I'm also extremely thirsty," he finally continued, grimacing as an elbow scored a direct hit on his spine. "Gayle! If you have any mercy in your soul at all, get me the hell out of this thundering herd!"

"Oh, dear!" Gayle's superior smile canceled her sympathetic tone. "Come along, boy genius, I know just the place."

The place Gayle led him to was a bar lounge on one of the store's many levels; Jake had stepped on and off the elevators so many times he had long since given up noticing what floor they were on. Fortunately, the place had one empty table, which Jake ruthlessly claimed as his own.

They were contentedly nursing their second round of drinks and nibbling on the small dish of snacks the waiter had placed on the table, when the light show began. From their vantage point overlooking the store's inner court, Jake and Gayle had an excellent view of the huge panel on which the display was presented.

There was a full range of holiday symbols, from Santa Claus right down the line to Rudolf, and tiny dancers, glittering snowflakes, bits and pieces from the Nutcracker, and, naturally, the enormous Christmas tree in all its bedecked splendor. The presentation was greeted with a chorus of oohs and aahs from the throats of hundreds of viewers jostling each other in their eagerness to see it. Even the sophisticated, world-traveled Jake was duly impressed.

That is, Jake felt he would have been duly impressed had he witnessed more than quick glimpses of it, which he sandwiched in between gazing at Gayle's enchanted expression. Before the fifteen-minute display of lights was half over, Jake felt as enchanted with Gayle as she so obviously was with the show.

"Wasn't it beautiful?" she asked dreamily when the show ended.

"Very," Jake agreed, smiling indulgently at the faraway look on her face. "I'll have to bring the girls to see it sometime."

"The girls?" Gayle arched one brow haughtily, banishing the dreamy look. "Which . . . girls?"

Jake's rumble of satisfied laughter drew reciprocal smiles from the patrons at nearby tables.

"My daughters," he chided, still chuckling. "The two we've spent a good portion of my hard-earned money on . . . remember?"

"The only information you offered was age and sex." Gayle sniffed. "Not once did you see fit to mention the fact that we were shopping for your daughters!"

Jake frowned. "I assumed you knew!" he exclaimed in self-defense. "Why in the world would I put myself through that human meat grinder down there"—he indicated the mass of people visible from their table—"except for my own daughters?"

"Jake!" Gayle's tone had an edge of exasperation. "I didn't know your children were girls!"

"Oh." Jake's frown deepened. "I thought I mentioned it." His eyes narrowed. "And, if I didn't, I certainly assumed Charley or Brant had!" It was an effort, but Jake contrived to look contrite. "I'm sorry, Gayle. Allow me to clarify. I have two daughters, ages seven and six."

"Really?" Gayle's eyes softened perceptibly. "Tell me all about them, Jake," she pleaded. "Please."

At that moment, Jake would have willingly told her anything she wanted to know, but he wanted to do it in an atmosphere more conducive to conversation.

"Not here," he said, shaking his head. "Over dinner, in a blissfully quiet restaurant." He smiled ruefully. "Where I can hear myself think."

Now, many hours removed from that blissfully quiet restaurant, remembering how swiftly Gayle had blazed a trail through the shuffling mass of shoppers to the pavement, Jake sipped his drink and smiled with satisfaction.

An excellent day's work, he congratulated himself.

Gayle had nibbled on the lure of his children as hungrily as she'd nibbled on the snacks provided by the waiter in the bar. Tossing the remainder of his drink down his throat, Jake set the glass on the credenza and sauntered into the bedroom. Yes indeed, he mused, stretching lazily, his plan was working beautifully.

Melissa and Deborah. Missy and Debbie. Seven and six. Perfect. Gayle sighed contentedly.

Drowsy, yet too keyed-up to sleep, Gayle sat curled into the window chair, dreamily reliving the incredibly enjoyable day and evening she'd spent with Jake Munger . . . of all people!

Never would she have believed that behind those rough-hewn features lived a man capable of such warmth, and consideration, and sheer mischievous deviltry. And if the shopping expedition had been fun, the evening had been both enlightening and rather romantic.

Smothering a yawn, Gayle laughed softly to herself. Never would she have believed she'd catch herself thinking of Jake as romantic! Yet, toward the end of the evening, that was exactly what he had been!

Gayle's laughter softened into a wistful smile as she remembered the way Jake had donned the mantle of proud father during dinner.

"All right," Gayle said with unabashed eagerness. "You're seated in a quiet restaurant." The movement of her hand encompassed the large, dimly lighted room, and the secluded table they had been shown to. Her glance indicated the glass in his hand. "You have a pre-dinner drink in your hand. Now, tell me about your daughters."

Jake's slow smile excited a familiar sensation in every nerve of Gayle's body. Hiding her reaction to him behind her fluted wine glass, she sat forward attentively.

"Okay," Jake began slowly. "Melissa is seven, Deborah is six. Missy is in the second grade, Debbie is in first." He paused to grin at her. "They are both beautiful, unlike their father. They are both very bright"—the grin widened—"very much like their father."

Jake's eyes grew cloudy, and Gayle realized that although he was looking at her, he no longer saw her.

"Go on," she coaxed softly.

"It's amazing how two sisters can be so very different," he went on absently. "Missy is a little lady, an absolute doll. Whereas Debbie, the little devil, is a rough-and-tumble hell-raiser, a dyed-in-the-wool tomboy." He smiled with heart-wrenching longing. "I adore them both, and I miss them like hell."

Gayle sat quietly while Jake took a long swallow of his whiskey. Then she probed softly, "They are still in California?"

"What?" Jake muttered. Then focusing on her, he nodded. "Yes." His lips twitched wryly. "In the now famous Silicon Valley."

Recalling the news articles she'd read, Gayle said, "Your plant's out there, isn't it?"

"It was." Jake responded immediately, but so very sharply that Gayle decided it prudent to steer clear of that particular subject. Whatever his reason, Jake's tone made it clear he would not relish questions on his business.

Backtracking, Gayle pursed her lips. "Now, let me guess. The Cabbage Patch doll is for Missy . . . right?"

"Right." Jake's smile brought a silent sigh of relief whispering through Gayle's lips.

"So the luge sled is for Debbie . . . correct?"

"On target." Jake laughed. "And I'll probably rue the day I gave in to her pleading for one!"

"And, of course, the Victorian-ruffled, red velvet dress is for Missy, while the ski pants and jacket are for Deb." She lifted one eyebrow. "Still on target?"

"Bulls-eye," Jake agreed. Then he frowned, oddly. "Why did you call her Deb?"

Now Gayle frowned. "I don't know. Why? Do you object to the diminutive of the diminutive?"

"On the contrary." Jake switched on his million-kilowatt smile, electrifying Gayle in the process. "I call her Deb myself. Strangely, I'm the only one who does call her Deb. I like it."

Inordinately pleased by his disclosure, Gayle drifted through the rest of their conversation somewhere in the vicinity of cloud nine.

Cloud nine proved to be a barren wasteland in comparison to the realm she discovered in Jake's embrace while dancing with him later.

With misgivings and much trepidation, Gayle had

allowed him to talk her into going dancing. As Louis was not fond of dancing, she had not set foot on a dance floor in over three years. And even in her twenties, Gayle had never considered herself the greatest of dancers. So it was a very timid Gayle who preceded Jake into the dark, smoke-filled club he escorted her to.

The table they were shown to was minuscule and dangerously unstable-looking. After seating herself gingerly, Gayle groaned aloud when Jake immediately got to his feet and held out one hand in invitation.

"I'm really not very good at this," she warned him, for perhaps the eighteenth time since he'd announced his intentions.

"But that's the beauty of this place," Jake purred into her ear. "If you will note the postage-stamp-size of the floor and the number of couples on it, you will realize how unnecessary it is to do any real dancing at all."

Guiding her onto a tiny section of the floor, Jake clasped her wrists, drew them around his waist, and, circling her neck with his arms, began swaying in time to the music.

It was at this point that Jake became romantic.

"Gayle, honey, will you relax?" he murmured, brushing her temple with his lips.

Gayle didn't have to make any effort; Jake's endearment drained all the starch out of her spine. Beginning to feel slightly boneless, she tightened her arms and allowed her body to flow into his.

"Yes, beautiful," he encouraged. "Just like that."

Sliding his hand under her hair, he gently massaged the sensitive area at her nape, drawing her face into the curve of his neck. "Lord!" he breathed. "You always smell so good."

"So do you." Gayle sighed, inhaling the scent of him.

"You feel good too." His other hand glided along the length of her spine, drawing her body into close contact with his. "Soft, and warm, and . . ."

"Fully packed?" Gayle finished for him.

"Nicely rounded," Jake corrected her tenderly. Raising his head only far enough to gaze into her eyes, he scowled fiercely. "You are not too fully packed," he declared with conviction.

"I've always longed for a figure like Charley's." Gayle sighed again.

"You long to be pregnant?" Jake teased.

"That, too," Gayle admitted, unaware of the sudden dullness in her eyes.

"Someday, darling," Jake crooned, rocking her gently in time to the wailing sound of a ballad. His hand moved from her nape to her waist, locking them together in an embrace. "You are still young."

"Thirty-three isn't young!" Gayle exclaimed, shaking her head moodily.

"Yes, it is," Jake insisted. "And so is the night. So, be quiet and enjoy."

"I am!" Lifting her head, Gayle gazed up at him, an element of surprise shimmering in her eyes. "I really am enjoying myself!"

"I'm glad." The smile that curved Jake's lips turned Gayle all soft and mushy inside. "You see," he scolded tenderly. "Courting is rather pleasurable . . . isn't it?"

"Hmmm." Gayle rested her head on his hard-muscled shoulder. "Dancing with you is, too. I'm not required to do any fantastic footwork."

Gayle felt the movement of his laughter through his body. "You're not required to do anything but be pliant in my arms." Jake's warm breath feathered the hair on the top of her head, sending shivers of delight cascading down her deliciously warm body. "But you are fantastic," he added huskily, tugging her hair gently to raise her face to his.

It was so unhurried, so natural, Gayle gave herself to his kiss without hesitation. Though Jake's lips hardened on hers, he made no demand. It was a testing sort of kiss, a mobile reconnaissance of her mouth without invasion. Strangely, Gayle was both thrilled and disappointed with his foray. She appreciated the pleasure she received from it, yet longed for more . . . much, much more.

Jake's uneven, ragged breathing when he released her mouth was a fair indication that he would have preferred more also. "This could become habit-forming, Gayle," he groaned in a rough whisper. "Not just kissing you, but feeling you close to me, holding all the sweetness of you against my body."

"Jake, I . . . I . . ." Gayle was experiencing sensations she'd never felt before, not even with Louis, and they frightened her in some inexplicable way. Jake made explanations unnecessary.

"I know, sweetheart. I know." His eyes soft with understanding, Jake smiled down at her then, loosening his hold as he inched back. "You're not ready for me yet," he said cryptically. "But don't worry about it, I can wait."

A slight sound—part sigh, part moan—whispered through the stillness of Gayle's bedroom. Stirring restlessly, she blinked and stood up slowly. Had she been dreaming, or merely daydreaming? A smile softened her kiss-swollen lips. How very gentle Jake had been, and how very considerate.

After hours of swaying as one on that tiny dance floor, he had brought her home, walked her to the door, and declined her invitation to come in with a brief shaking movement of his head.

"You're tired," he'd murmured against her lips. "And I'm not certain I can trust myself." His mouth brushed hers—once, twice—and then he groaned. "God! Gayle, in all honesty I must admit that I want you something fierce!" His arms tightened spasmodically, crushing her to him for an instant. Then she was set free and Jake stepped away from her. "Go inside, Gayle. Sleep well. I'll call you in the morning."

Sleep well! Gayle drifted to her bed like a disembodied spirit, sat on the edge, and hugged herself happily. She'd be lucky if she could sleep at all!

Jake Munger was proving more potent than the headiest of wines! Still hugging herself, Gayle stretched out on the bed. Her eyes widened with a sudden, startling realization.

Though Jake still frightened her, he now excited her more!

Chapter Eight

During the following two weeks Jake came "a-court-in'" nearly every evening. He kept Gayle in a state of breathless anticipation by squiring her all around town, and sometimes out of town as well.

They attended the symphony, the ballet, and a pre-Broadway play that was currently running in Philadelphia. They spent one weekend in Atlantic City—with never a suggestion of anything but separate rooms—where they took in three altogether different and altogether delightful shows. But Jake's pièce de résistance was the excellent seats he'd acquired for a performance by Lucianno Pavarotti at the Met.

Although Louis had always indulged her, never in her adult life had Gayle received such exquisite attention from a man. And that man was, at all times, a gentleman. Not once in those weeks did Jake ask for more than an undemanding good-night kiss.

By the second weekend after their shopping spree, Gayle and Jake were talking and laughing together like old friends, and the fear that had gripped Gayle at their initial meeting was slowly receding into her subconscious.

On the Saturday of that weekend Jake showed up at Gayle's door late in the afternoon, his arms laden with the packages she'd helped him select, plus all the paraphernalia necessary to gift-wrap them.

"But Jake!" Gayle cried, bemoaning the helplessness of most males. "Why didn't you have them wrapped in the store?"

Jake was wrapped rather sexily himself in faded jeans that caressed his hips and long legs lovingly, a teal-blue cableknit pullover, and a suede jacket that had to have worn a price tag of several hundred dollars.

Standing in the middle of the clutter, Jake contrived a look of astonishment while grinning wickedly.

"And cheat you out of the opportunity to help me?" he exclaimed with a wounded air. "I wouldn't do that to you, Gayle."

Restraining a smile with difficulty, Gayle breathed a long-suffering sigh. "You're all heart, Mr. Munger."

Jake's grin went from wicked to lecherous. "Well, not quite *all* heart, Ms. d'Acier," he assured her in a gravelly whisper. "Would you care to see proof?"

Used to Jake's particular brand of teasing by now, Gayle raised one hand and yawned delicately behind it. "I think I'll pass, thank you." Scooping up one of the shopping bags, she started to walk away. Then, smiling over her shoulder, she said, sweetly, "I'll forego the lesser excitement in favor of the real thrill found in wrapping gifts."

"You're a cruel woman, Gayle." Grumbling, Jake collected the rest of the packages and followed her into the dining room. "Here I've been spending a fortune wining and dining you, and what do I get in return?" Dropping the bags and boxes of assorted sizes, he planted his hands on his slim hips. "I'll tell you what I get . . . potshots at my manhood!"

"Did I do that?" Gayle fluttered her lashes innocently—a trick she'd learned from observing Charley for years, but had never tried herself. "How very clever of me!"

"One of these days I'll show you clever," Jake mumbled in a mock-threatening tone. Moving to assist her in clearing the table of its centerpiece and lace cloth, he slanted a narrow-eyed glance at her. "I'll show you clever until you beg for more."

For an instant, Gayle went cold all over, fearfully searching his expression for a hint of latent cruelty. What she found was a still watchfulness.

"I'll never deliberately hurt you, Gayle." Jake gazed into her guarded eyes with forthright steadiness. "Never," he repeated firmly. Straightening to his full height, he stared across the table at her a moment. Then a conciliatory smile softened his hard mouth. "And you can take that to the bank," he teased in an obvious attempt to ease the tension tautening her body.

Gayle smiled back tremulously. "Your"—she

paused to wet her parched lips—"your word is that safe, is it?" she managed to tease.

"Blue chip, honey." Moving slowly, carefully, Jake walked around the table to her, gazing down at her out of eyes tender with concern. "Fourteen carat." Raising one hand, he smoothed the worry line between her brows. "It was a man, wasn't it?" Jake's voice had an odd, raspy sound.

Gayle didn't pretend not to understand. "Yes," she admitted softly.

"The bastard."

Gayle caught her bottom lip between her teeth at the note of cold contempt in Jake's tone. Though his contempt was not aimed at her, it was chilling nonetheless.

"It was a long time ago." Gayle was only partially successful in making her shrug seem careless. "I should have forgotten the incident long ago. I don't know why I didn't."

With sudden clarity and amazement, Gayle heard the truth in her words; she really should have put the incident behind her years before! Why had she kept the memory alive? she wondered. Uncannily, Jake seemed to answer her silent question.

"You were protecting yourself." Jake smiled at her blink of surprise. "Nothing unusual in that, honey," he assured her gently. "It's no longer necessary." His features were set in lines of determination. *"I'll* protect you from now on."

Yes, but who will protect me from you? Gayle sighed regretfully at her own lack of faith. Jake had given her his word, and still she doubted.

"Would it help if you talked about it, Gayle?" Even as she began to shake her head in denial, he added, "Turning a light on banishes the shadows, honey."

"I know, but . . ." Gayle frowned. "Why do you call me honey?" Her query was not simply a ruse to change the subject; she really wanted to know.

"Because you are a honey," Jake chuckled. *"My* honey."

"Jake . . ." Gayle drew his name out warningly.

Grinning unrepentantly, Jake turned back to the table. "I think we'd better get started here. I'll wrap, you decorate." Sliding a fat roll of embossed paper out of a bag, he waved it aloft. "Okay?"

Gayle smiled her defeat. "Okay. Where are the decorations?"

"In the white plastic shopping bag," Jake murmured distractedly, measuring the paper against a box. "And would you also fill in the tags? This one's for Deb."

For the next two hours they worked together in complete harmony, Jake wrapping neatly, Gayle decorating creatively. When all the gifts were finished and placed carefully inside the shopping bags, Jake stood back from the table with a groan.

"I must be getting old," he mused aloud. "I feel as if my back's broken."

"How old are you, Jake?" Gayle asked, grasping the opportunity to learn something personal about him.

"Thirty-nine," he answered frankly. With a knowing smile, he arched one brow. "Anything else you'd like to know?"

Gayle hesitated, then blurted, "Why don't you want to talk about your business?"

"Because the details still rankle," Jake said roughly. "But if you give me a sandwich and a bottle of beer, I'll tell you the whole sorry story."

"A sandwich!" Gayle exclaimed. "Do you mean we're not going out to eat?"

"You got it, honey."

"But I gave Marge the night off!"

"And there's nothing to eat in the house?" he inquired, too innocently.

"Oh, I'm sure there's plenty, but . . ."

Jake smiled contentedly. "Let's go raid the fridge."

Without waiting for a response, Jake strode into the kitchen. Gayle was left with little choice but to follow him, and she quickly found that when Jake said *raid*, he meant exactly that.

Laughing together, they assembled a hot and cold supper; the hot being soup from a can, and the cold the weirdest sandwiches Gayle had ever eaten. When Jake made a sandwich, he put everything that didn't crawl in it!

Happily munching away on the surprisingly delicious concoction, Gayle coaxed, "Okay, you have your beer and sandwich, now tell me the whole sorry story."

Jake took a long swallow of his beer, studying her over the rim of the glass. "Have you heard of greenmail?" he asked, placing his glass on the table.

"Yes, a little. Isn't that the practice of buying up shares of stock in a mock takeover for the purpose of selling the shares back to the company at an exorbitant price?"

"Close enough," Jake said grimly.

"It happened to your company?" Gayle breathed in disbelief. Jake nodded. "But, what did you do?" she demanded.

"I paid it," he said simply. "Then I sold the business."

Gayle stared at him in amazement. "But what are you going to do now?"

The hard set of Jake's jaw relaxed as he smiled. "I don't *need* to do anything, Gayle. All the assorted Mungs have made me a very rich man. I could retire."

The slight emphasis he'd placed on the word "could" was a giveaway. "But you're not going to?"

"No, I'm not going to," Jake answered. "I'm going to build a new plant here, in Pennsylvania." He shrugged. "I've been thinking about coming home for some time." His gaze ran over her like warm seawater. "Now I'm glad I made the move."

Feeling her cheeks glow with pleasure, Gayle cleared her throat. "Will you locate your plant in the Philadelphia area?"

"No." Jake shook his head. "I'm looking at a site near Lancaster."

"Oh." Gayle lowered her eyes to conceal the sharp pang of disappointment that twisted through her. "And the house you were looking at the week before Thanksgiving, is that near Lancaster too?"

"Not too far away," Jake admitted, scrutinizing her expression. "I'd like you to see the house. Would you drive out there with me tomorrow?"

Gayle fidgeted with her napkin, sipped at her beer, then, giving in to curiosity, murmured, "Yes."

Early the next morning, Gayle and Jake drove to the property he'd taken an option on the week of Thanksgiving. Unfamiliar with the area, Gayle knew only that it was situated somewhere between Ephrata and Lancaster on the crest of an incline that overlooked the undulating patchwork of farmland.

Gayle loved the house on sight. Tudor in design, it was large, with leaded windows and an overall effect of welcoming warmth and safety from any storm.

Wandering through the empty rooms, Gayle caught herself mentally furnishing them with period pieces, imagining how they would look with the windows draped by sheer panels billowing in a spring breeze. Jake said little during the tour. It was not until after he'd guided her outside for a stroll down to the man-made lake on the property that he asked softly:

"Well, what do you think of it?"

"It's beautiful." Pausing beside a starkly leafless tree, Gayle smiled at him. "But you didn't need me to tell you that."

"No, I didn't." Bending over, Jake picked up a pebble, then sent it skimming over the surface of the lake. Not looking at her, he continued, "But I wanted your opinion." Turning, he gave her a quizzical look. "Do you think the girls will like it here?"

"What a question!" Gayle laughed. "Jake, I don't know your girls, but really, I can't imagine any child not being entranced with this place."

"What about any woman?" Jake asked soberly. "You in particular?"

Now Gayle turned away to gaze out over the gently rippling water. "Jake, I . . . I don't know, I . . ."

"Look at me, Gayle," he murmured urgently. When she'd complied, he cupped her face in his hands. "The house is mine; I received word from the agent on Friday. All we have to do is set a date for the closing. I'd like it to coincide with the date I set with you."

"Date?" Gayle swallowed with difficulty. "What date?"

"You know what date!" Lowering his head, Jake kissed her softly. "I'm asking you to marry me, Gayle."

Though Gayle tried, she couldn't swallow at all now. Inside, a war raged, fear and desire the opposing forces. Unable to think straight with his mouth hovering over hers, Gayle slipped out of his grasp and walked slowly along the edge of the lake. Jake paced beside her silently, patiently.

When the tension started to crackle between them and she still didn't respond, Jake began speaking in a tightly controlled voice.

"Don't close up on me, Gayle. And don't close me out. I gave you my word that I'd never hurt you." Stopping suddenly, Jake curled his fingers around her arm, turning her to face him. "Do you believe me? Do you *trust* me?"

"Yes." As she uttered the word, Gayle realized it was true. When had she begun to trust him? she wondered, watching as the strain eased from his features. Gayle didn't know, but then, it really didn't matter. "Yes," she reiterated, "I do trust you, Jake. But is trust enough?"

Suddenly, for Gayle, Jake's answer was the most important thing in the world. For, suddenly, Gayle realized that *Jake* was the most important thing in *her* world. Jake didn't make a pretense of ignorance.

"I don't know if I love you, Gayle," he said with gentle bluntness. "I do know I care for you—deeply." Sliding his hand around her neck, he drew her close to his body. "I know it feels right when I hold you in my arms. I know I want you to belong to me completely." Sighing, he closed his eyes and lowered his head to rest his forehead against hers. "But I can't honestly say that what I feel is love. I don't know if I believe in the emotion; I do know that I don't trust it." When he lifted his head, his eyes were cloudy with memories. "You're not the only one who's been hurt, Gayle."

For some incomprehensible reason, Gayle found a vulnerable Jake more upsetting than a frightening Jake. Rising on tiptoes, she placed a kiss at one corner of his mouth. She gazed up at him with eyes softened by compassion. "Your wife?" she asked gently.

Jake's entire body stiffened, and Gayle felt positive he would refuse to answer. Then he expelled a long, harsh sigh and nodded.

"Yes, my wife." A derisive smile twisted his lips, causing Gayle to feel a burning resentment against a woman she didn't even know.

Gayle examined the emotions racing through her mind and body. There was anger for Jake's ex-wife;

there was jealousy for her, too, and for every woman Jake had known since; but, primarily, there was all-encompassing love for this man she'd been almost terrified of a brief two weeks before; and, finally, there was sadness for herself, and the man who no longer believed in love.

"I'm . . . I'm sorry," Gayle whispered.

"What for?" Jake's eyes caressed her cold-reddened cheeks. "You didn't do anything."

"I know." Gayle lifted her shoulders in a helpless shrug. "But, I'm a woman, and . . ."

"There's no comparison, Gayle!" Jake's sharp tone cut across her attempt at explanation. "You're all soft, and warm, and pure female." His eyes grew stormy again. "Melanie was all hard, and cold, and pure bitch."

"But you married her, Jake!" Gayle cried, hating the very idea of his being attracted to the type of woman he'd described.

"Oh, yes, I married her." His harsh laughter contained more mockery than humor. "It's a long story, and . . ." Bending, he brushed her cheek with his parted lips. "Damn!" he growled, jerking his head back to stare at her closely. "Your face is as cold as ice!" Cursing under his breath, he moved far enough away from her to shrug out of the pile-lined suede jacket he was wearing.

"Some big-deal protector I turned out to be!" he rasped, wrapping the jacket around her shoulders. "Come along, darling." Pulling her close to the warmth of his body, he started walking to the house. "I've got to get you warm!"

Startled by his abrupt action, bemused by the sincere sound of his endearment, Gayle allowed herself to be hustled along beside him.

"I'm all right, Jake!" When all she got in response to her assurance was another string of muttered curses, Gayle closed her mouth and quickened her step.

Jake paused at his car long enough to withdraw a plaid lap blanket, shaking his head when Gayle asked in surprised confusion if they were going back to the city.

"There's kindling and logs for a fire," he informed her soothingly. "I'll get one going at once."

The cold stillness of the house was even more penetrating than the outside air. Teeth chattering, Gayle stood shivering as Jake wrapped her inside the blanket.

"B-B-But, Jake! At least take your jacket back!" she protested.

On one knee at the fireplace, Jake shook his head. "I'm fine," he insisted distractedly, busy with the kindling. When the fire was going well, he placed a log carefully in its center, and only then turned back to her. "Besides," he continued as if there'd been no span of time at all, "if I take my jacket back, I'll have no reason to share the blanket with you." The grin he tossed her caused goose bumps that had nothing to do with the cold. Gazing at her over his shoulder, he motioned for her to join him with a slight movement of his head. "Come sit by me where it's warm," he coaxed softly.

Unhesitatingly, Gayle went to him. As she moved to sit down, he jackknifed to his feet.

"Wait a minute!" he cautioned. "Let's do this right."

Loosening the blanket, he removed his jacket from her shoulders, spreading it on the floor, pile side up. After helping her down, he sat beside her and drew the blanket around them both.

"Now, isn't that better?" he whispered close to her ear, encircling her with both his embrace and the blanket. "Are you warming up?"

What a question!

"Gayle?"

"Hmmm?"

"I asked if you were warm." Jake nuzzled the sensitive area behind her ear.

Sighing with contentment, Gayle shifted herself closer to his hard body. "Beautifully warm," she murmured, shivering with excitement as his breath feathered her skin. "Are you?"

"I think I passed warm a few minutes ago," he admitted. "But the base of my spine is beginning to complain."

"Oh! I'm sorry!" Gayle stirred as if to get up.

"Relax, sweetheart," Jake murmured. "I'll take care of it."

Gayle felt him remove one arm, but, as the other arm held her clasped to his side, she had no idea what he was doing until she felt herself being lowered gently to the floor.

"Jake!" she yelped, trying to sit up.

"It's all right, honey. There," he crooned, settling her on the fleecy pile. Propping his head with one hand, he leaned over her. "Isn't that more comfortable?"

Comfortable, yes, Gayle acknowledged silently. Entirely safe? Gayle thought not . . . but, she was warm, and getting warmer by the second!

Gazing up at him, she was struck by the harsh beauty of his face, his tan all coppery-looking in the flickering glow from the fire. Her breath catching in her throat, Gayle realized there was a matching flame in his eyes that was not a reflection, but came from a fire deep inside him. Beginning to feel as if she were melting from the heat scorching her, Gayle sought frantically for something to say.

"You were telling me about your wife!" she blurted.

For an instant Jake stiffened. Then, sighing softly, he smiled. "Ahh, yes." He sighed again, heavily. "My wife."

Settling himself more comfortably on his side, very close to her, Jake glanced into the dancing flames. "I met Mel nine years ago, not long after the first Mung was marketed. I had been working nonstop for what seemed like forever, and I was unknowingly at the point of exhaustion."

He paused, a sad smile curving his lips as he stared into the flames mesmerized, as if watching his memories unfold. When he began speaking again, his voice was so low Gayle had to strain to hear him.

"She was so very beautiful." Jake's smile twisted sardonically. "And I was so very hungry."

"Hungry?" Gayle prompted when he grew quiet once more.

"What?" Jake dragged his gaze from the flames to frown at her. "Oh, yes. I was hungry. Hungry for action. For life. For anything! I had spent upwards of eighteen hours a day developing that damned thing, and after that I had to push like the devil to get it on the market." Jake shook his head as if he pitied the thirty-year-old he'd been. "If I was exhausted, I was also exhilarated. I'd worked so long . . . so hard. I wanted to celebrate. And Mel was beautiful. And willing."

Gayle closed her eyes against the look of pain etched harshly on Jake's face. Feeling his pain inside her own body, she raised her hand and slid her fingers over his lips.

"Jake, please stop!" she whispered urgently. "It's not necessary."

Catching her hand with his, Jake kissed her fingers, then her palm. A shudder ran the length of his body as he teased the soft skin with his tongue, a shudder that was echoed in Gayle's now limp body.

"I think it is necessary," he disagreed. "Very necessary." Keeping her hand captive inside his own, he went on. "I thought she wanted the same things I did—a home, children, a deep, caring relationship, commitment." Drawing her hand higher, he kissed the fluttering pulse at her wrist, smiling in satisfaction when Gayle made a low, moaning sound in her throat.

"Anyway"—Jake expelled his breath harshly—"I convinced myself Mel loved me, just as I'd convinced myself I was in love with her." He moved his shoulders uneasily. "Hell, if you believe you're in love, it's the same as actually *being* in love—isn't it?" He stared down at her.

Was it? Gayle wondered foggily. Bemused by the movement of his lips against her palm, enveloped in the warmth of his nearness, Gayle was too far gone to consider the truth of his statement. She felt about ready to burst into flames that would put the ones in the fireplace to shame.

Apparently, Jake was every bit as bemused as Gayle. Sliding his elbow along the floor, he stretched out beside her.

"Where was I?" he murmured close to her ear.

"You were . . . in"—Gayle swallowed—"in love . . . you thought."

"Love," he repeated in a tone so sensual that Gayle's toes curled inside her shoes. "I want to make love to you, Gayle."

Gayle shivered as Jake's lips glided across her cheeks, the tip of his tongue leaving a trail of fire. "You were"—she had to pause to gulp at a shallow breath—"you were telling me about your marriage."

"Oh, hell!" Lifting his head, Jake scowled at her. "Will you let me kiss you after I finish?" he asked outrageously.

Let him! Gayle smothered a bubble of laughter. She couldn't wait! "If you insist," she said demurely.

"Oh, I certainly do," he assured her seriously. "Okay. I'll make it short and bitter. Mel *didn't* want the same things I did." Again he shrugged, this time uncaringly. "I don't know, maybe, in her own strange way, she did love me—at least in the beginning. But she wanted to run and play . . . continuously. I was delighted when she became pregnant a few months after we were married. Mel hated it. And she barely looked at Missy when she was born."

Though Gayle could see that Jake was trying to keep his face free of expression, the hurt defeated his efforts.

"At first, Mel's attitude toward Missy merely cooled my ardor. But, when she continued to ignore the baby, she turned me off." His lips twisted with self-loathing.

Without thinking, Gayle asked the question that zeroed in on the cause for his self-contempt.

"But Deb!" she exclaimed. "You mean she isn't yours?"

"Oh, yes," Jake sighed. "She's mine—as you'll see when you meet her. She looks like me . . . in a soft, feminine way."

"But, Jake, I don't understand! If your wife turned you off, then how—"

"I'm a man, Gayle!" Jake said bluntly. "A man with a driving need to succeed, and a sexual drive that equals it. I wouldn't consider infidelity. So, when the need outweighed my better judgment, I went to her." Jake laughed, nastily. "At least I did until she became pregnant with Deb. After that, I went without."

Turning her head, Gayle stared into the fire, aching for him, chastising herself for raking up the past. Jake's long fingers caught her chin to ease her head back to where he could watch her expression while he finished his story.

"In retaliation, Mel packed up and left after Deb

was born, taking my babies with her." Jake's tone when he said "babies" sent a knifing pain into Gayle's heart. "That was her mistake. I would have remained faithful, supported her, given her anything she wanted, as long as she remained in *my* house, caring for *my* children." His eyes narrowed in memory. "She cut her own throat by trying to take my kids from me."

"What—what did you do?" Gayle wasn't even sure she wanted to know.

"Exactly what I did with the greenmailer," he said grimly. "I paid her off and told her to get lost. I haven't seen or spoken to her in five years. She has no visiting rights; that stipulation was part of the divorce settlement."

They were quiet for a long time after Jake stopped talking, each of them deep in his own thoughts.

She had been right about him, Gayle concluded. Jake *was* ruthless. But, she temporized, only when provoked. Longing to ease his pain, or share it, or merely just comfort him, Gayle slid her arms around his muscle-tautened neck and drew his face to hers.

"Sympathy, Gayle?" Jake murmured tauntingly against her lips.

"Yes," she admitted honestly.

"I'll take it," he groaned, covering her parted lips with his own.

As before, Jake's kiss was gentle and undemanding. Wanting something more, yet not knowing quite what that something was, Gayle moved closer, then still closer to the warmth radiating from him.

Jake's fingers caressed her cheeks, her ears, and her

shoulders restlessly. When her body jerked from a force searing her from the inside out, he pulled his hand away and rolled onto his back.

Breathing heavily, he whispered urgently, "I can't take much more of this." Turning his head, he stared at her through stormy eyes. "Marry me, Gayle."

Gayle lowered her lashes.

"When?" she asked, and answered him at the same time.

Chapter Nine

A silent bystander would have found it difficult to decide which of the two was more surprised, Jake or Gayle herself. For seconds that stretched into minutes, they lay still, staring into each other's eyes, sublimely oblivious to the incongruity of the scene.

Enveloped in a warm world of their own making, they were not conscious of the penetrating cold that permeated the empty rooms in the large house, or the darkness of late afternoon settling like a mantle over the landscape, or even the dusty hardwood floor. They lay there, not touching, yet connected by the humming wire of awareness that stretched between them.

"Jake?" Gayle said anxiously, breaking the spell by blinking.

"Ssh, don't rattle me," Jake whispered theatrically. "I'm already in a state of shock."

Trying not to laugh, Gayle mimicked his tone. "Is that anything like the state of confusion?"

The lines at the corners of Jake's eyes deepened with amusement. "No." He shook his head decisively. "You have to travel through confusion before you reach the state of shock." Sliding his hand from her shoulder to her face, he outlined her bottom lip with his finger. "Correct me if I'm wrong, but you *did* say yes . . . didn't you?"

"Yes, Jake. I did say yes." Gayle smiled into his gleaming eyes. "Well, actually, what I said was—when?"

"Would you mind being rushed a bit?" Now Jake sounded anxious.

Ignoring the twinge of renewed panic at the outer limits of her consciousness, Gayle drew a deep breath, then plunged into irrevocable commitment. "Not if there's a good reason," she said. "Is there?"

"I think there is." Jake's voice trailed away as his gaze dropped to her mouth and the continuing action of his finger. "I need to kiss you."

Although the feeling of panic expanded, Gayle was past the point of noticing. The rawness of Jake's voice, combined with the erotic play of his finger against her lip, had set her blood racing through her veins like a flash flood. The sudden demands of her body dictated her response.

"Then do it."

Jake did, but again so very gently that Gayle had to

squash a desperate urge to grasp his head with her hands and crush his mouth to her own. She was filled with the rage of a desire unlike anything she'd ever experienced before in her life. Closing her eyes, she tried to sort out her feelings.

Without a shred of doubt, Gayle knew she was in love with Jake, deeply in love. Yet, she'd loved Louis too. So, then, why was this new love different? The sexual relationship she and Louis had shared had been good and mutually satisfying. Yet, never had she felt gripped by an overwhelming need to possess and be possessed such as she was feeling at this moment.

This new longing to meld with, actually become a part of, another person was both confusing and scary.

"Gayle, honey." The tight sound of Jake's voice drew her attention, and she gazed at him out of thought-clouded eyes. "Have I frightened you?" Giving her no chance to reply, Jake enfolded her in the haven of his arms. "I'm sorry, sweetheart. It's just that I'm so relieved, so . . ."

"You didn't finish telling me why you want to rush into marriage," Gayle interrupted him teasingly, unable to bear the uncertainty in his voice; the mere idea of Jake's being uncertain about anything was practically beyond belief!

Jake rubbed his nose against hers. "You mean besides wanting to slip my ring on your finger before you have a chance to change your mind?" he murmured, an odd seriousness interwoven with amusement in his tone.

Gayle gave him a distinctly dry look.

Though Jake shook his head in despair, he didn't

challenge her dubious expression. "I would like to present the girls with a fait accompli when they arrive from the west coast," he explained.

Although a cold finger of unease slid the length of her spine, Gayle asked calmly, "Are you trying to tell me to be prepared for their resentment?"

Jake's expression of shock was obviously genuine. "Of course not!" Shock gave way to a devilish grin. "They have been bugging me for over a year to get married and settle down."

Gayle's unease now had a different source. "Do I deduce from that remark that up till now you've lavished your attention on a vast number of ladies?"

Jake frowned, but answered chidingly, "I've been a free agent for over five years, Gayle. And, yes, there have been women. But certainly *not* vast in number . . . and"—his tone hardened—"I was not serious about any one of them. Any other questions?"

"One," Gayle answered in a small voice.

Jake eyed her suspiciously. "And that is?"

"When *do* the girls arrive from the west coast?"

The laughter that rumbled through Jake's chest instilled a sense of peace in Gayle.

"You do enjoy throwing me off balance, don't you?" he chuckled. "The girls are due at Philadelphia International on the twenty-first," he went on.

"But Jake!" Struggling out of his arms, Gayle sat up, staring at him in amazement. "The twenty-first is only two weeks away!"

"Do tell?" he teased, folding his hands behind his head and staring back at her. "I did mention the word rush . . . didn't I?"

"Two weeks?" Gayle repeated numbly.

"Two weeks," Jake echoed firmly.

Two weeks. Curled up once again in the chair by the window, Gayle heard the words revolve inside her mind. Two weeks. Two weeks. Two weeks.

Moving restlessly, she stared through the pane at the blackly outlined branches of a murmuring blue spruce.

What had she let herself in for? she asked the star-studded sky beyond the wind-tossed branches. But, more important, could she go through with it? Raising a hand to her throat, Gayle drew deep breaths while monitoring her pulse rate.

Fluttery, to say the least, she decided, grimacing at her lack of confidence. What *was* she afraid of, anyway? she mused. Jake had not at any time displayed a tendency toward brutality. Quite the opposite. In all ways, he had shown her nothing but gentleness and consideration. But, by his own admission, Jake was capable of ruthlessness. So, in effect, there was a beast lurking inside the man.

Despite a moan of protest, the old memory surfaced. Pressing herself back into the chair's soft padding, Gayle moved her head from side to side as she relived the terror of a thirteen-year-old girl.

"Nonsense!"

Jumping to her feet, she strode to the bed, yanking the covers back impatiently. Hadn't she admitted to Jake that she should have put the memory from her long ago? Climbing into bed, Gayle nodded her head sharply once. She had, and she would. Hadn't she also assured him that she trusted him? Again Gayle's head moved briefly. She had, and she did.

So, she was nervous. So what? Weren't all women nervous about getting married? Of course they were. Closing her eyes determinedly, Gayle continued her silent pep talk. And what do women do when they're nervous? They keep themselves as busy as possible. And that is exactly what you are going to do, Gayle d'Acier. You are going to keep yourself so busy you won't have time to think, let alone agonize over something that happened to an immature girl twenty years ago.

Two weeks. Stretching lazily on the bed, Jake savored the sexual thrill that zigzagged erratically through his long body. Only two weeks to get through before he'd see the culmination of his plans.

A wry smile curving his lips, Jake sighed softly into the quiet, darkened room. Of course, his plans had altered slightly along the way, he mused, not dissatisfied with that alteration. Quite the contrary. Having set out to acquire a suitable mother for his daughters, Jake considered himself fortunate in having found a more than suitable life partner for himself. A partner, moreover, upon whose body he had such delicious designs!

His own body beginning to ache, Jake brought his erotically meandering mind up short. Gayle is still afraid, he cautioned himself sternly. Keep it together, Munger. And keep it gentle, or you will lose her.

That thought chased the warm sensuality from his body, replacing it with a chilling emotion very like fear. You *could* still lose her, his conscious mind warned, even now. Becoming rigid, Jake examined the possibility, and found it valid.

Gayle could, on reflection, decide not to take a chance on the man who—how had Brant phrased it?—had a raw look about him. Frowning, Jake lifted one hand and rubbed it over his whisker-bristled face. But dammit! I'd never hurt her, he swore mutely. I care for her too much!

For endless minutes Jake lay still, his body taut with tension. Then, reaching a decision, he slowly relaxed. He wouldn't give her time to reflect, and possibly change her mind. In fact, he mused determinedly, he'd keep Gayle so damned busy during the next two weeks she'd hardly have time to think at all . . . let alone reflect!

One week to the day after she'd agreed to marry him, Gayle and Jake exchanged vows, and rings, in the presence of Jake's family, Charley and Brant, who acted as witnesses, and the pastor of the church Jake's mother and father attended.

As soon as the bride and groom had kissed, the gathering moved en masse out of the confines of the pastor's small office. Piling into vehicles of assorted shapes and sizes, they drove the short distance to the Mungers' big, old-fashioned farmhouse, where a few friends and neighbors waited to fete the bride and groom.

For Gayle, already tired from the hectic pace Jake

had set for her throughout the week, the entire day blended into a blur of impressions.

She had wakened to the sound of light tapping on her bedroom door, and Marge's equally light voice.

"It's seven-thirty, Gayle. Time to rise and shine if you want to be ready when Charley and Brant arrive."

Mumbling under her breath, Gayle rolled over and went back to sleep—for all of five minutes. The shrill ring of her bedside phone jolted her back to wakefulness.

"Good morning, sweetheart." Jake's voice poured over Gayle like warm honey. "Were you awake?"

"Yes . . . well, almost," Gayle admitted. "Marge knocked on my door a few minutes ago." Although she tried to cover it by placing her palm over her mouth, Jake's chuckle told her he'd heard her yawn.

"Tired, honey?" he commiserated softly.

"Of course I'm tired!" Gayle yawned again, noisily. "You've been running my . . . ah . . . legs off all week."

Jake laughed, excitingly, deep in his throat. "But it was worth it, wasn't it? The closing's over with. The decorators are busy carrying out your instructions. And all your Christmas shopping is finished," he said, verbally ticking off the list of their week-long marathon of activities.

"Don't remind me," Gayle groaned, only half in jest.

"But now the worst is over," Jake said soothingly. "All that's left is the ceremony and the small reception my folks have planned, and then we can both rest till the twenty-first."

"And I just might sleep the entire seven days," she muttered wearily.

"Then again, you just might not," Jake murmured, sexily, before adding briskly, " 'Bye, love, see you in church."

Charley and Brant arrived at the house several minutes earlier than the time agreed on, brimming over with smiles and good wishes . . . as indeed they had been ever since Gayle had announced her intention of becoming Jake's wife.

Fortunately, Charley chattered happily throughout the drive to the church, which was located near Ephrata, making all but the most trivial responses from Gayle unnecessary.

Now, glancing around the large living room of her new in-laws' house, Gayle made an attempt to at least appear alert. Smiling gratefully, she accepted a glass of champagne from her new brother-in-law—the good-looking one named Richard—and turned to listen to what her other new brother-in-law—the youngest of the three sons—was saying to her.

Finally, when it seemed to Gayle that the babble of voices would never end, Jake came to her, his murmured words echoing her thoughts.

"Let's escape from this cuckoo's nest. After this, I really *need* a week of rest and quiet." Slipping his arm around her waist, he drew her with him to the door.

After the cacophony of laughing voices saying good-bye, the hum of the car's motor was music to Gayle's ears. Settling into the plush upholstery, she sighed deeply, content to make the entire drive back to Jake's hotel in companionable silence. Jake had other ideas.

"I thought it went rather well, didn't you?" Slanting a quick glance at her, he raised one eyebrow.

"Hmmm." Gayle nodded.

"Charley and Brant were certainly obvious about their delight with the whole thing, weren't they?" he persisted.

"Hmmm." Gayle didn't even bother nodding.

"Have you had too much wine?" Jake shot her another look.

"No, of course not!" Gayle came alive. "I was merely drinking in the quiet."

Jake grinned at her unrepentantly. "Mother and Dad like you," he went on, undaunted. "In fact, I think it's safe to say that the whole blessed Munger clan, down to the youngest of the gaggle of nieces and nephews, likes you."

"I'm glad." Gayle smiled. "Because I like all the Mungers too."

"One of which you are now, even as we speak," Jake teased. "So look alive, new Munger, we have arrived at our home away from home." Gayle and Jake would be staying at his hotel until the work on their new home was completed.

The way Jake bustled her out of the car and into the hotel, Gayle barely had time to become nervous. That is, until the door to the suite was closed and locked behind them, and she found herself standing in the center of the bedroom, frantically swallowing to ease the sudden tightness in her throat.

"It's all right, Gayle," Jake said softly from his position against the door. "I'm not going to pounce on you." Opening the door, he moved to stand in the threshold. "You have a warm bath and unwind. I'll go down to the bar and have a drink and a cigarette."

Startled, Gayle spun around to stare at him quizzically. "But, Jake, you don't even smoke . . . do you?"

"No." Jake shrugged, then grinned. "I'll pretend."

The door closed softly and he was gone, leaving Gayle with the distinct impression that she was behaving like a twit.

Will you grow up? she chastised herself, retrieving the sheer nightgown she'd purchased on impulse while shopping for the cream wool dress she'd chosen to be married in. Closing the dresser drawer Jake had allotted her, she marched into the bathroom.

Pink-skinned from a long bath and clad in the knee-length gown, modestly covered by a belted, ankle-length velour robe, Gayle was standing at the bedroom window when the door was opened quietly behind her. Forcing herself to move slowly, she turned, eyes widening at the sight that met her gaze.

His hair still wet from the shower, Jake stood framed in the doorway, his long, raw-boned frame only partially covered by a cinnamon-colored, midthigh-length terry robe.

"But how . . ." Gayle sputtered.

"This suite came complete with two bathrooms," Jake explained, walking slowly to her. "When I came back after finishing my drink and found you were still in the tub, I grabbed my robe and made use of the extra shower." Coming to a halt mere inches from her, he smiled. "You look . . . warm," he said softly, raising his hands to the knot in her belt.

Swallowing visibly, Gayle gazed up at him pleadingly. "Jake . . . I . . . I . . ."

Cursing quietly, Jake pulled his hands away as if the material had scorched him. "Dammit! Gayle, enough is enough!" Wheeling away from her, he took two steps, then swung back to face her, his features set with determination. "I want you to tell me about it." Pure steel ran through his tone.

"Jake, please! I've never told anybody!" Gayle protested.

"Then it's time you opened the door to that musty room in your mind and let some fresh air in," Jake decreed flatly.

Aghast, Gayle stared at him a long time. Then, certain he would torment her until she told him everything, she began talking in a monotone.

"It happened the summer I was thirteen. I was sunbathing by the pool on the grounds behind my home. I thought I was alone." As a vision of her attacker rose in her mind, Gayle's voice became high-pitched and ragged. "A shadow cooled my skin, and when I opened my eyes to find the cause of it, he was standing there, his eyes crawling over my body." Gayle's voice faltered as remembrance sent a shudder through her body.

"He was a stranger?" Jake's voice was carefully controlled; Gayle didn't notice.

"No." She shook her head distractedly, not even aware that Jake was leading her to the side of the bed, but grateful to sit on the edge and clamp her shaking knees together.

"Go on," Jake prompted, sitting down beside her and taking her hands in his.

"I'd met him before." Gayle grimaced. "He was a friend of my mother's."

"Did he rape you?" The iciness of Jake's tone brought gooseflesh to Gayle's arms, and she glanced at him fearfully.

"No!" She moistened her parched lips nervously. "My mother arrived home before he could . . ." She drew a deep breath. "But he hurt me. He kissed me so brutally he cut the inside of my lip and . . . and he thrust his hateful tongue into my mouth." Again Gayle paused for breath. Then she went on, hurriedly. "I fought him; kicked him, tore at his hair. He cursed me and pulled the top of my bikini suit down to grab my breast."

Unconsciously, Gayle raised her arms, crossing them protectively over her chest. Unaware of her action, she could only wonder at the sudden shimmer of hate in Jake's angry green eyes.

"Then he clawed at the bottom of my suit," she went on, her eyes shying away from his frightening expression. "That was when my mother came home. Before he let me go he warned me never to tell anyone. I never did. For weeks I had to hide the bruises that covered my left breast and hip."

"The son of a . . ."

"But the bruises weren't what caused the worst

pain, Jake," Gayle cried over his snarled epithet. "Or even the terror I'd felt while he was pawing at me."

Drawing air deeply into his chest, Jake looked at her, a frown furrowing his brow. "What do you mean? If that wasn't the worst, what was?"

"Oh, I admit that since then I've had an unreasonable fear of men, but . . ." She shrugged helplessly. "Jake," she continued more calmly, "that man didn't tear away just my swimsuit. He tore the veil of innocence from my eyes. With his brutality he made me aware of what was going on around me, and I loathed him for that more than the attack." Groping her way, Gayle moved on toward the light at the end of the dark, twenty-year tunnel.

Her expression one of growing wonder, Gayle gazed up at him in amazement. "Jake, it's not only the physical brutality I fear in men," she said slowly, "but their psychological brutality as well!"

Grasping her by the shoulders, Jake turned her to him. "Gayle, honey, I don't understand." There was a strange, almost scared note in his voice. "Other than the psychological scars naturally inflicted by an attack of that kind, how could he have hurt you?"

"He made me aware!" Gayle cried. "Dammit, Jake, he made me *see* that he and my mother were lovers! I could barely bear being around her after that day, and I had adored her! But, even worse than that was watching my father, knowing he knew inside and refused to face it!" Hot tears ran unheeded down her cheeks, and she sobbed. "Oh, God! Why are men such beasts?"

"Cry, darling." His voice suspiciously thick, Jake

slid his arms around her trembling body and drew her close to his own strength. "Cry for your lost mother. Cry for your father. But, more importantly, cry to free the woman from the pain inflicted on the child."

Rocking her, stroking her back, Jake murmured soothingly until the purging storm had abated. When Gayle was all cried out, he dried her face, then handed her a tissue from the bedside table, smiling as she blew her nose.

Physically tired, emotionally exhausted, Gayle could utter no more than a feeble protest when Jake stood her up and removed her robe.

"Easy, honey," he murmured soothingly. "All I'm going to do is make you comfortable." Pulling back the spread, and then the blanket and sheet beneath it, he continued, "You're worn out and you need rest." Lifting his hand slowly, he fingered the lace edging on the gown that revealed more than it concealed of her full but firm breasts. "A pity," he muttered so softly that Gayle wasn't even sure she heard him correctly. "You'd tempt a saint in that little bit of nothingness, and I sure as hell never aspired to canonization."

Long past the point of resistance, Gayle stood limply, staring up at him with eyes shadowed by weariness.

"God! If I could get my hands on him, I'd strangle that . . ." His voice going low, Jake rattled off a string of obscenities that sent color rushing to Gayle's cheeks.

In contrast to his vicious tone, Jake's hands were amazingly gentle as he lifted her, then carefully laid her in the middle of the bed. Silent and wide-eyed, Gayle watched as he shrugged out of the terry robe. Even in her near-catatonic state, she couldn't help admiring the masculine magnificence of his muscular, raw-boned, unadorned body. Yet, when he slid that naked body onto the bed next to hers, Gayle stiffened with apprehension.

"Relax, honey, relax," he crooned softly, drawing her rigid body close to his warmth. "I don't attack little girls. I'll wait for the woman to emerge."

Gayle frowned uncomprehendingly. What was Jake talking about? Too tired to decipher his meaning, she snuggled closer to his hard chest, sighing in appreciation of the light stroking of his hand down her back. She was asleep within seconds of closing her eyes.

Gayle woke several hours later, disoriented but, amazingly, rested. She began to move, then froze, frowning at the feel of silky whorls of hair against her cheek.

Louis?

In the same instant that the name flashed into her mind, it was pushed out again by another one.

Jake!

Fully awake now, Gayle lay still, remembering the night before, and the hysteria she'd succumbed to. What must Jake think of her? she wondered despairingly. She had agreed to marry him, to be, in every way, his wife. Then she had cheated him out of his conjugal rights on his wedding night!

Her face warming with shame, Gayle closed her eyes and moved her cheek lightly over his chest.

Behind her lids moisture welled, and she sniffled delicately. The scent that filled her nostrils was intoxicatingly musky, and all male.

With the scent came a vision of the brief glimpse she'd had of Jake, his body beautiful in nakedness. Now the heat flowing under her skin was caused by an altogether different reason.

Obeying an age-old urge, Gayle moved with unconscious sensuality against him, exquisitely conscious of the exciting contrast between his male hardness and her feminine softness. His sudden tautness made her aware of his wakefulness an instant before he brought his hand to her chin to lift her face to his.

"Welcome back, woman," Jake whispered, his seagreen eyes smiling into hers.

A tiny line marred her brow. In a corner of her mind Gayle knew Jake's odd phrasing was connected to something he'd said to her moments before she'd drifted into oblivion, yet she couldn't quite put her finger on exactly what it was. Then, as he drew her mouth to his, it no longer mattered.

"Please, don't be afraid of me, darling," he murmured against her lips. "I promise you I will never do anything to hurt you."

"I know that, Jake," Gayle whispered.

"Louis was your only lover?" he asked raggedly in a tone that conveyed conviction rather than question.

"Yes."

"And he was . . . gentle?"

"Yes," Gayle repeated distractedly, entirely missing the slight hesitation in his voice.

"Then I will be more gentle still," Jake vowed, all hesitation gone.

With soft words and tender hands, Jake proceeded to make good his promise.

When Gayle woke again, it was to full daylight, and an even fuller realization that she was Jake's wife entirely.

Chapter Ten

Gayle and Jake spent most of that week in the true honeymoon tradition, closeted together away from the everyday worries of the world, getting to know each other as only two people who share a marriage bed can.

During that week, Gayle learned that Jake was excessively neat, due to the strict training of a loving but—in Jake's own words—"tough" mother.

Among Jake's discoveries about Gayle was her "scandalous"—again in his words—propensity for sleeping late in the morning, which was due to her habit of going to bed very late at night.

Their knowledge of each other expanded to include their intellectual and emotional selves, as well as their dreams and desires.

And, while Jake made exquisitely gentle love to her body, Gayle came to know all the hard, muscular angles of his.

The week was restful, and peaceful, and should have been satisfyingly fulfilling for Gayle, but confusingly, a part of her remained empty. Though she pushed all speculation as to what was lacking in their relationship to the furthest edges of mind, there were times, late in the night after Jake was deeply asleep, that Gayle would mentally probe at the cause of her discontent, wondering if the cause lay within her or her husband.

Like all moments out of time, their honeymoon week ended much too soon.

It was not until the morning of the twenty-first, mere hours before the plane carrying Jake's children was due to land, that Jake finally broached the question of Gayle's career.

"Are you . . . completely dedicated to the law?" he asked quietly, his pause brief but telling.

"And if I say yes," Gayle responded softly, forbidding the understanding smile that flirted with her lips, "will it cause our first marital argument?"

"No argument," he said resignedly. "I think you are all too aware that I'd prefer to have you remain at home as a full-time wife and mother but"—he paused to shrug—"if your career is important to you, I will not object."

Coming from Jake, the concession was staggering, as was his use of the word "wife" before "mother." He had been brutally frank from the outset about his desire for a certain type of woman, one whose main function would be that of full-time mother to his children.

Allowing the flirting smile to have its way, Gayle revealed even, white teeth prettily.

"The law is not the be-all and end-all of my life, Jake," she told him honestly. "Actually, I find it rather dull and dry." Struck by sudden insight, she paused, then said wonderingly, "You know, I believe I deliberately chose the law because it represented a shield for me to hide behind!" Her smile widened with warmth. "As I no longer need the shield, I'd be delighted to make a career of keeping your house and children."

"And me too," Jake chided.

"And you too," Gayle laughed easily. "Just as long as you behave yourself.

In truth, Jake behaved himself very well. With seemingly effortless ease, he stepped into whatever role he was called upon to play, whether it was husband, father, son, friend, or inventive genius.

Even though Jake had informed the girls of his plans to marry, and had subsequently introduced Gayle to them via telephone, Gayle fully expected at least a few moments of awkwardness when they met face to face.

But thanks to the ease with which Jake executed the reintroductions, not a hint of awkwardness marred the happy reunion of father and daughters. With a thoughtfulness that pleasantly surprised Gayle, Jake gave his daughters the freedom to question both him and their new mother, and requested they extend the same courtesy to Gayle.

To her delight, Gayle found the girls exactly as Jake had described them. Missy looked the perfect little lady, a legacy, Gayle felt sure, from her beautiful mother. And, amazingly, Deb *did* resemble Jake in a soft, feminine way.

The personalities of both girls were endearing, and within hours of the girls' arrival Gayle knew she liked them very much. Not too surprisingly, after several weeks of living with them, Gayle knew she had lost her heart forever. She adored the children every bit as much as she had come to adore the father.

For the first time in twenty years, Christmas was a joyous occasion for Gayle. The happy laughter of children, *her* children, completed the circle of love that surrounded the traditional holiday celebration.

As the holidays passed and the bleakness of January lay over the rolling Pennsylvania farmlands, Gayle found herself with little time to be affected by the inclement weather. Her days were full, her nights were serene.

Even with the girls in school and Jake away from home most days poring over designs for the new plant, Gayle was seldom idle for any appreciable amount of time. When she had told Marge about her intention to marry Jake and move into his house, Marge had promptly announced her own intention of accompanying her—with Jake's approval, of course.

As Jake's approval had been immediate and warm, Marge was in residence as housekeeper. And, much against Jake's approval, Gayle and Marge, working happily together, kept the big house running like clockwork and spotlessly clean.

If at unexpected times Gayle probed at the sore spot of emptiness deep inside, she did so with the full knowledge of all the blessings that were hers.

And so, it was a basically happy Gayle who woke on a Saturday morning at the end of January to the realization that she didn't have to do anything, not even move, if she didn't want to.

Deciding that Gayle needed a break from the rigors of new motherhood *and* housekeeping, Jake had taken matters into his own hands. He had sent the girls to his parents, and Marge to her brother and sister in-law in Philadelphia for the weekend.

Stretching luxuriously, Gayle settled back into the warm covers to enjoy her freedom and contemplate her renewed life. Within minutes she reached the conclusion that she was better off not thinking too much.

Stirring restlessly in the long, wide bed, Gayle pinpointed the cause of her vague uneasiness. The empty spot inside her was demanding to be recognized. And this time there were no diversions; even Jake seemed to have disappeared for the moment.

Jake.

Merely thinking his name caused a shiver to run down her spine.

Jake.

Envisioning the man behind the name caused an ache that slowly expanded to encompass her entire body.

Jake.

How very much she loved him!

Gayle grew still, listening to what her emotions were trying to say to Her. Her eyes closed, her breathing shallow, Gayle slowly absorbed the message.

How could she love him, more than her own life, and still retain an empty spot? Jake had never said he loved her. Would hearing him say the words fill that emptiness? Gayle rejected the idea without examination. Jake had proved himself to her a hundred, a thousand, no countless times over. If it took him years, or if he never said the words, it wouldn't matter; Jake was hers, and she knew it.

Was she, then, still afraid of the beast she believed lurked in every man, ready to leap forth when it became hungry enough? Gayle moved her head vigorously back and forth on the pillow; if there was a beast inside Jake, he had it controlled by a very firm leash.

Listen, listen, she told herself urgently. Becoming still once more, Gayle listened to her mind and to her heart, and then she knew. As clear as if he were standing next to her, Gayle heard the words Jake had said to her on their wedding night.

"I'll wait for the woman to emerge."

And then again, his voice, early the next morning.

"Welcome back, woman."

And then again, his voice, a little later.

"Louis was gentle? I'll be more gentle still."

"No!"

Startled at her own outcry, Gayle shot into a sitting

position. It was not fair! Of all men, Jake deserved more, much more than she had offered him!

Tears gathered in her eyes—tears of shame for herself, tears of sympathy for Jake—as Gayle looked at their situation realistically for the first time. And what she saw made her cringe, for although she had never physically denied him, she had never once encouraged him, either.

If *she* had an empty spot, she concluded contritely, Jake must be living with a chasm.

Regret made her tears fall more quickly.

And that was how Jake found her when he walked into the room with a cup of coffee and a good-morning smile. The sight of the tears running down her face wiped away the smile and filled his eyes with sharp concern.

"Gayle?" Crossing the room with several long strides, Jake deposited the cup on the bedside table and bent over her, his hand capturing her chin to raise her lowered head.

"Honey! What's the matter?" Frantic eyes danced over her face looking for clues. "Are you ill?"

"No." Lifting her hand, she dashed away the tears. "No," she repeated strongly. "I'm not sick, I'm stupid!"

"What?" Frowning, Jake sat on the edge of the bed, his hip touching hers. "You're not making sense, Gayle."

"Nothing new about that!" She laughed derisively, then sniffed. Easing her chin from his hand, she reached for a tissue from the box on the night table. As she mopped her face and blew her nose, her eyes came to rest on his body, enticingly uncovered by the same short terry robe he'd worn on their wedding night. She mused on how the cinnamon color brought out the auburn highlights in his hair . . . and the woman in her.

As he'd slid onto the bed the robe had parted, revealing one long, muscular thigh resting close to her hip, the tanned, taut skin inviting her stroking fingers. Gayle accepted the invitation.

Tentatively, then boldly, she stroked her hand the length of Jake's thigh, thrilling to the sound of his sharply indrawn breath.

"Gayle?" Jake's whisper had an ache in it. Encouraged by the sound, Gayle glided her hand up and under the robe, her breath catching when he groaned, "Oh, God, Gayle! Darling, don't stop! You'll never know how much I've longed for you to touch me . . . oh, Lord, yes, just like that!"

Shrugging the robe from his body, Jake flung it carelessly to the floor. Gayle's nightgown followed an instant later. Then, drawing her against his chest, he lowered her to the bed. And still, Jake's hands caressed her with infinite gentleness.

At long last, the woman rose from the ashes of fear. And suddenly wild for him, Gayle stole the initiative from his gentle grasp.

Clasping Jake's head in her hands, Gayle speared her fingers through his hair, tugging at the silken strands to draw his mouth down to hers.

Jake's raspily growled "God, yes!" were the only words he had time to speak before Gayle's hungry lips greedily demanded active participation from his.

Boldly engaging his tongue in a sensual duel, she slid her hands to his neck and then sent them skimming the length of his broad back, fingers teasing, nails leaving faint marks on his smooth, hot skin.

Her frenzy heated Jake's blood; her love assault drew forth the warrior in him. The erotic battle was on. A battle that would end with no losers, only winners.

With eager hands, and seeking tongues, and writhing bodies, they grappled in fierce pleasure, each determined to deal the other the ultimate blow of supreme ecstasy.

By the time Jake joined with Gayle in a clash of bodies, their breathing was labored. The harsh, ragged sounds they made were the music for their ancient ritual of possession . . . hers and his.

When Gayle woke, it was late afternoon. Jake still slept deeply beside her. Moving cautiously to relieve her cramped muscles, she discovered not unpleasant aches in several key portions of her anatomy.

Savoring the memory of their lovemaking, Gayle also made two far more important discoveries. The first one was that the empty spot was now filled. The second one was that the fear she'd lived with for twenty years was gone.

She was free!

Smiling contentedly, Gayle ran her hand caressingly over Jake's body from his shoulder to his hip, reveling in his strength, no longer afraid of waking the hungry beast inside.

Not that there wasn't one. There most assuredly was! But, she qualified silently, placing her lips to his warm chest, the beast was a love tiger, easily tamed by willing lips and encircling arms and soft, clasping thighs. Gayle now recognized the beast in Jake, for a female beast lived inside her as well.

"Darling?" Gayle called softly, relishing her first use of the endearment.

"Hmmm?" Opening his lids a mere slit, Jake gazed down at her out of glittering eyes the color of emeralds.

"Do you want to fight . . . again?"

The spring sunlight was warm on Gayle's upraised face. Lulled by the swish of water lapping at the soil around the lake, she rested back on her elbows, basking in the warmth like a lazy cat.

It was Saturday afternoon, the day before Mother's Day, and exceptionally warm for early May. A ripple of girlish laughter wafted over the water to Gayle, and, lifting her eyelids slightly, she smiled. Missy and Deb were out on the middle of the lake in an inflatable rubber boat, in the care of their fourteen-year-old cousin, Rick. Jake and Rick's father Richard, Jake's older brother, were off checking on the progress of the new plant Jake was having built less than thirty miles from the house.

Mother's Day. Sighing contentedly, Gayle rolled the phrase around in her mind. *Mother's Day*. Although it was supposed to be a big secret, Gayle knew the girls were planning something special for her in celebration of the day. A soft chuckle tickled Gayle's throat. From the whisperings and gigglings the past week between the girls and Marge, she would have had to be unconscious not to know there were secret goings-on in the house; Missy and Deb had even gotten Jake into the act!

Gayle's smile grew dreamy as she thought of Jake, and she moved one hand protectively over her abdomen. Next year there would be a bigger celebration on Mother's Day, she mused, rubbing the still almost imperceptible bulge gently. As always, the feel of the growing mound sent a thrill racing through Gayle's entire body.

Not even six full months to go anymore! Gayle exulted, sure she'd burst with happiness if she wasn't careful. And the realization that she'd conceived Jake's child on that fantastic Saturday morning in January when she'd finally and forever cast off her fears made her happiness doubly satisfying.

"Hey! Gayle!" Deb's squeaky young voice called to her. "Are you asleep? We've been waving to you for five minutes!"

Easing herself up, Gayle shaded her eyes and waved to the three youngsters floating peacefully on the lake. Resting her arms on her knees and her chin on her arms, Gayle allowed her lids to drift closed again.

How extraordinarily wonderful her life had become! Gayle marveled. Within the short span of four months she had leaped the invisible barrier between fear and loneliness to contentment and happiness!

Her husband was thoughtful and attentive . . . and a spectacular lover! His children were hers . . . even if they did call her Gayle instead of mother. She was thirteen weeks into her first pregnancy. What more could any woman ask for—without appearing exceptionally greedy?

Drifting in the nether world between sleep and wakefulness, Gayle was indulging in the game of "who will the baby favor, Jake or me?" when a frightened scream pierced her daydream, and a splash sent her eyelids flying wide.

Without conscious thought, Gayle was up and running, taking a quick glance at the little boat as she ran. Deb was struggling within Rick's confining hold, her voice high-pitched with terror as she called instructions to her sister, who was floundering wildly in the water.

Missy! A shaft of fear shot through Gayle. Unlike her younger sister, who swam like a little fish, Missy could barely stay afloat doing the dog paddle!

At the edge of the lake, Gayle slipped out of her loafer-style flats before dashing into the water. The shock of the spring-fed lake water against her ankles was numbing, yet Gayle kept on until the water swirled around her knees.

"Paddle, Missy!" she shouted. Then, drawing a deep breath, she propelled her body forward, flat out in a shallow dive; the impact of the icy water chilled Gayle's sun-warmed body to the bone.

Hypothermia! She had to get Missy out of the freezing water! Her arms fought the weight of her wet clothes, pulling her body through the water with a strength born of fear. On and on Gayle plunged, unmindful of the paralyzing cold.

In actual time the entire rescue took mere minutes. In Gayle's fear-ridden mind, it was a long, living nightmare. Ever afterward she would remember the sequence of events from the moment she heard Missy scream till she'd carried the child into the house as a confusing blur.

Certain moments stood out from the blur with stark clarity, like freeze-frame shots in a movie that was being run on fast forward. There was the frame of grasping Missy, the blur of towing her to shore. There was the frame of wrapping the sobbing, shivering child inside the blanket Gayle had been sunbathing on; the blur of issuing orders to Rick and Deb. There was the frame of carrying Missy to the house; the blur of feeling her limbs complain and her lungs heave for breath. There was the frame of Marge, rushing up the stairs before her; the blur of tearing at Missy's wet, clinging clothes. And there was the frame with dialog; the blur of Jake striding into the child's bedroom.

"Gayle! What the hell hap . . ."

"Jake, I can't get her wet jeans off!" The frantic voice was Gayle's own. "Dammit! Help me!"

With Jake's entrance the nightmare quickly reached its conclusion. Missy's jeans flew off her trembling legs and into a corner. The child was lifted off her feet and placed lovingly into the warm bathwater Marge had run into the tub. And then Gayle herself was swept into those strong, capable arms.

"Richard!" Jake's bark held sharp command.

"I'm ahead of you, Jake!" Richard's reply came from the master bedroom.

Shaking, teeth chattering, Gayle was carried into the bathroom. She was barely conscious of her brother-in-law as he directed a concerned glance at her on his way out.

"Jake!" Gayle's weak protest at the way Jake was tearing her clothes from her body lacked authority.

Intent on his task, Jake didn't even look at her. "I've got to get you warm," he growled without a hint of apology.

Then it was Gayle's turn to be submerged into deliciously warm water. Sighing with relief, she lay unresisting as Jake sent the chill from her head by applying the hand spray to her hair.

The worst of the chill was gone, but Gayle was still shivering when Jake hauled her out of the tub and rubbed her body down briskly with a terry bath sheet. Carrying her into the bedroom, he slipped a nightgown over her head, bullied her into her velour robe, then proceeded to dry her hair with the blow-dryer. Jake was wielding the brush effectively, if inexpertly, when Richard strode into the room with a steaming cup of heavily sweetened tea. Gayle heard their exchange as if from far away.

"Missy?" Jake asked tersely.

"Dry and warm, and guzzling a cup of hot chocolate," Richard comforted. "How's Gayle?"

"Almost out of it," Jake replied less tightly. "I'm going to pour this tea into her, then let her sleep." There was a pause, during which Gayle gulped the drink held to her lips. When Jake continued speaking, she was already half asleep. "Then I'm going to pray both she and the baby are all right."

Gayle was wakened by something cool tickling her face, and the scent of lilacs filling her senses.

"Hmmm," she murmured, slowly raising her eyelids. "How lovely."

The picture that met her fully opened eyes would remain indelibly imprinted on Gayle's mind and heart for the rest of her life.

Missy and Deb, their adorable little faces solemn with concern, stood side by side next to the bed. Jake sat on the edge of the bed alongside Gayle's hip, his eyes mirroring his daughters' concern, an enormous bunch of lilacs clutched in one long hand.

"Happy Mother's Day, Mommy." The girls' greeting held a hopeful note. "Are you . . . better?" Deb added tremulously.

Mommy. Enthralled, Gayle stared at the girls, a tightness closing her throat for a moment. Then the events of the day before flashed into her mind. Jerking up onto her elbows, Gayle examined Missy's face with a probing look.

"Are you feeling all right, honey?" she asked anxiously, grasping the covers to throw them back. Jake's free hand halted her exit from the bed.

"Missy is fine." His calm tone meant more than the verbal assurance. "Except," Jake went on teasingly, "for her worrying about you. She and Deb have been begging me to wake you for over an hour. I only gave in because I was every bit as worried as these two monkeys are." He smiled wryly. "I might add that Marge is running a very close fourth."

"But I'm perfectly all right!" Gayle smiled. "As a matter of fact, I feel wonderful!"

The relief expressed on the faces of father and daughters was nearly palpable. Gayle's throat closed completely with emotion. Blinking against tears, she gazed lovingly at each of their faces, settling on the one that filled her heart to overflowing. The sea-green eyes said everything that ever had to be said about love, in all its forms.

His gaze piercing her soul, Jake spoke to his daughters in a revealingly hoarse voice.

"I think you gals have a surprise to get together, don't you?"

Two pair of eyes began to shine with excitement.

"Ohmigosh!" Deb ran the phrase together in her sudden fluster. Missy gave a yip, and covered her mouth with her hand.

"What's going on?" Gayle teased as the girls spun on their heels and dashed for the door.

"You keep Mommy here till we call you," Deb instructed Jake excitedly. "Okay, Dad?"

"Okay, Deb," Jake agreed seriously, his eyes inviting Gayle to share his parental enjoyment.

"Hey!" Gayle accepted his invitation gratefully. "Why am I being confined to my room?"

"It's a Mother's Day surprise for you." Missy delivered the explanation in her prim, ladylike voice as she stepped into the hall.

"Yeah! We're cooking breakfast for you all by

ourselves," Deb said, revealing the secret with heart-warming artlessness.

Jake's bark of laughter almost concealed Missy's scolding cry.

"Deborah!"

Gayle joined Jake in laughter as the bedroom door closed, muffling Missy's tirade. Jake's amusement vanished as if the click of the closing door had been a signal.

"I want to thank you for the gift of my daughter's life." Jake's voice had a suspicious tremor. "Even though I must admit that it would have been a bittersweet gift, if it had been purchased at the cost of the life that means more to me than any other single thing on this earth."

"M-Mine?" Gayle just managed to whisper the word before her heart appeared to stop beating.

"Yours." Jake's beautiful eyes were a sea of turbulent feelings. "Gayle, if I were to lose you now, it would cripple me emotionally." Bending to her, he kissed her tenderly. "I told you once that I didn't believe or trust in love." Drawing a deep breath, Jake blinked against a shimmering wetness in his eyes. "That was before I learned what love was all about."

"And"—Gayle had to swallow to continue—"and what is love all about, Jake?" Ignoring the tears spilling over her lids, Gayle raised her fingertips to brush at his wet lashes.

"It's about being together in the truest sense of the word. A sharing of everything, spiritually and physically. Laughter, warmth, sadness, passion," Jake blinked unashamedly. "And even tears when necessary. Had it not been for you, I never would have known this joy called love." Lifting his hand to her face, Jake gently wiped away her tears. Then, in the most simple, yet most effective way possible, Jake gave voice to his commitment.

"I love you, Gayle." Crushing the bouquet of lilacs between them, he sealed his pledge with his lips. "You feel the same, don't you?" The conviction in his tone made a statement of the question.

"Yes." Though soft, Gayle's voice held equal conviction. "I love you, Jake. And feel exactly the same way. Loving you has driven all the dark shadows from my world." Smiling gently, sniffing softly, she added, only half-teasingly, "And brought the scent of springtime into my life."

Jake's rumbled laughter had the sound of youthful eagerness; his kiss held a promise for all of their seasons together. His kiss was deepening when a call from the base of the stairs shattered the sensuality shimmering between them.

"Daddy! You can bring Mommy down now," Deb shouted at the top of her voice.

"Happy Mother's Day, Mommy," Jake murmured, splaying his long-fingered hand over her growing abdomen possessively and protectively.

"Come on, my love." Standing, Jake threw back the covers. "Let's go have breakfast with *our* daughters."

Silhouette Romance

COMING NEXT MONTH

NOTHING LOST—Laurie Paige
Donna Whitaker's pride held her together after Alex
Hofstedder left her waiting at the altar. Now he was back in
town, claiming to love her, and his devastating presence
threatened to crumble her resolve.

RELUCTANT BRIDE—Doris Lee
Vicky had been only sixteen when she first lost her heart to Jeff
Hudson. Now she was a woman, and Jeff wanted to marry
her…but for all the wrong reasons.

AN OBVIOUS VIRTUE—Arlene James
Gene Brannick was willing to love, but only on his terms.
Destry, with the help of her large, loving family, was
determined to teach him the art of give and take.

EYE OF THE WIND—Elizabeth Hunter
Caring for Bart Bennett's convalescing daughter seemed like a
good job for Jane Lister. Then she found herself caught
between her growing passion for her patient's father, and the
sudden reappearance of her mysterious mother.

MERMAID—Victoria Glenn
Diana Mueller was hauntingly familiar. Wasn't it her sultry
voice Chase had been hearing in his dreams? Diana held tight
to her secret, in spite of Chase's determined challenge.

WISH UPON A STAR—Cassandra Bishop
Jane Jones, professional image maker, had transformed
herself into a fashionable package. Astrophysicist Hank
Mosely had no use for facades. So why did he find himself
intrigued by the woman underneath the glitter?

AVAILABLE THIS MONTH

THE SCENT OF LILACS
Joan Hohl

ENTER WITH A KISS
Diana Dixon

RACE FOR THE ROSES
Maxine McMillan

THE TROUBLE WITH CAASI
Debbie Macomber

A WILDER PASSION
Karen Young

SOMETHING FOR HERSELF
Dixie Browning

WIN

a fabulous $50,000 diamond jewelry collection

ENTER

by filling out the coupon below and mailing it by September 30, 1985

Send entries to:

U.S.
Silhouette Diamond Sweepstakes
P.O. Box 779
Madison Square Station
New York, NY 10159

Canada
Silhouette Diamond Sweepstakes
Suite 191
238 Davenport Road
Toronto, Ontario M5R 1J6

SILHOUETTE DIAMOND SWEEPSTAKES ENTRY FORM

☐ Mrs.   ☐ Miss   ☐ Ms   ☐ Mr.

NAME _____ (please print)

ADDRESS _____ APT. #

CITY _____

STATE/(PROV.) _____

ZIP/(POSTAL CODE) _____

RTD-A-1

RULES FOR SILHOUETTE DIAMOND SWEEPSTAKES

OFFICIAL RULES—NO PURCHASE NECESSARY

1. Silhouette Diamond Sweepstakes is open to Canadian (except Quebec) and United States residents 18 years or older at the time of entry. Employees and immediate families of the publishers of Silhouette, their affiliates, retailers, distributors, printers, agencies and RONALD SMILEY INC. are excluded.

2. To enter, print your name and address on the official entry form or on a 3" x 5" slip of paper. You may enter as often as you choose, but each envelope must contain only one entry. Mail entries first class in Canada to Silhouette Diamond Sweepstakes, Suite 191, 238 Davenport Road, Toronto, Ontario M5R 1J6. In the United States, mail to Silhouette Diamond Sweepstakes, P.O. Box 779, Madison Square Station, New York, NY 10159. Entries must be postmarked between February 1 and September 30, 1985. Silhouette is not responsible for lost, late or misdirected mail.

3. First Prize of diamond jewelry, consisting of a necklace, ring, bracelet and earrings will be awarded. Approximate retail value is $50,000 U.S./$62,500 Canadian. Second Prize of 100 Silhouette Home Reader Service Subscriptions will be awarded. Approximate retail value of each is $162.00 U.S./$180.00 Canadian. No substitution, duplication, cash redemption or transfer of prizes will be permitted. Odds of winning depend upon the number of valid entries received. One prize to a family or household. Income taxes, other taxes and insurance on First Prize are the sole responsibility of the winners.

4. Winners will be selected under the supervision of RONALD SMILEY INC., an independent judging organization whose decisions are final, by random drawings from valid entries postmarked by September 30, 1985, and received no later than October 7, 1985. Entry in this sweepstakes indicates your awareness of the Official Rules. Winners who are residents of Canada must answer correctly a time-related arithmetical skill-testing question to qualify. First Prize winner will be notified by certified mail and must submit an Affidavit of Compliance within 10 days of notification. Returned Affidavits or prizes that are refused or undeliverable will result in alternative names being randomly drawn. Winners may be asked for use of their name and photo at no additional compensation.

5. For a First Prize winner list, send a stamped self-addressed envelope postmarked by September 30, 1985. In Canada, mail to Silhouette Diamond Contest Winner, Suite 309, 238 Davenport Road, Toronto, Ontario M5R 1J6. In the United States, mail to Silhouette Diamond Contest Winner, P.O. Box 182, Bowling Green Station, New York, NY 10274. This offer will appear in Silhouette publications and at participating retailers. Offer void in Quebec and subject to all Federal, Provincial, State and Municipal laws and regulations and wherever prohibited or restricted by law.